SWEET HOME JACKSON HOLE

CINDY KIRK

Waverly
House

ISBN: 9798362767679

First published in 2010 as THE DOCTOR'S BABY by Silhouette Books

CHAPTER ONE

Giving birth in an emergency room wasn't on July Greer's agenda. Neither was having her one and only one-night-stand be the doctor striding through the door.

Though a mask covered his mouth and nose, she'd have recognized those electric-blue eyes anywhere. For a second the pain and pressure gripping her body paled in comparison to her shock.

You're not supposed to be in Wyoming.

The accusation never made it to her lips. Another vise-like pain gripped her belly and she cried out.

"I'm Dr. Wahl." Without casting a glance her way, he rushed past her to take a seat at the other end of the exam table. He dropped out of sight for a moment then pushed the sterile drape down.

"We don't have time to get you to the delivery room." The tense set to his jaw and the concern in his eyes did nothing to ease her anxiety. Thankfully, if he recognized her it didn't show. "How far along are you?"

July prided herself on her even temperament, but the pain had taken over her body again and her temper flared. She'd given that information at the admissions desk and to at least two ER nurses. Couldn't one person have written it down?

"Thirty-six weeks." Her irritable tone morphed into a pant even as she fought to not bear down. The urge became overwhelming though the nurse standing beside her chanted in her ear that she must.not.push.

July vowed to stay strong, to pant like a dog for as long as it took to protect her baby. If only there was some guarantee her efforts would be enough. She wasn't due for a month. According to all the books, a baby did a lot of growing those last few weeks.

"He'll be okay, won't he?" July asked when she could breathe normally again.

David, er Dr. Wahl, must have heard the fear in her voice because he lifted his head. "If your dates are accurate, lung maturity shouldn't be a problem."

"Is that a yes?" July snapped as another sharp pain ripped through her body.

"The baby is crowning. Take a couple breaths, then hold and push," he instructed.

Though it seemed like an eternity, minutes later her son made his appearance, weighing in at a respectable five pounds two ounces.

The baby was carefully inspected before Madi Oliver, the RN who'd been at her side, brought him close. A check of fingers, toes and body parts confirmed that while he might be small, her son was indeed perfect.

The breath July had been holding came out in a whoosh. All the sacrifices she'd made these past eight months had been worth it. Gazing into his unfocused eyes she vowed that no matter how rough life got, she'd always be here for him.

She was only beginning to get acquainted with her new son when an RN July hadn't seen before swept into the room. With competent hands, she took him from her arms. "We're just taking him for a routine test. We'll bring him right back."

Despite the assurance, July's heart twisted as the baby disappeared from sight.

"You did fantastic." Madi squeezed her shoulder. "Don't worry about your little boy. We'll take good care of him."

Her little boy. The tidal wave of emotion continued to build. "His name is Adam."

July was sentimental when it came to names. Unlike her own, which was simply the month she was born, she wanted her son's name to mean something more.

"I like Adam." Madi rolled the name around on her tongue. "Is it a family name?"

July nodded. Adam "A.J." Soto was like a brother to her. Had been ever since they'd done the foster home circuit together. For as long as she could remember A.J. had been her confidante, her sounding board and most of all, a good friend.

"He certainly is a handsome boy with all that dark hair," Madi commented.

Lots of dark hair had been what July had noticed first about her baby. While she loved her reddish-colored hair, she was glad Adam's hair was more like his dad's.

"Does he look like his father?"

"He does." July spoke without thinking. She wasn't sure what David was "finishing up" down there but she felt him pause. Though she couldn't see his hair under the blue cap, she vividly remembered running her fingers through the dark wavy strands that long ago night.

The words had barely left her lips when he stood. With one gesture he brushed off the cap, lowered the mask and fixed his gaze on her. For the first time since he'd entered the room, he focused, *really* focused on her. Though it was barely noon, lines of fatigue edged his eyes. Yet a curious glitter shone in the blue depths.

A sense of danger snaked its way up her spine and she started to shake. If David discovered Adam was his son...

For a second the room spun but July refused to give into the fear.

You've gotten yourself out of worse.

The realization steadied her. She took a deep breath and forced the fear from her mind. One step at a time. That's how she'd managed to get through life so far and it was how she'd get through this unexpected calamity.

First, she needed to stay calm and not overreact. David had no reason to think their one night together had resulted in a pregnancy. That's how she intended to keep it.

"Everything looks good." His gaze never left hers. "The baby was small so despite the precipitous delivery, you didn't tear at all."

Perhaps she should have been embarrassed by the comment, but David was a doctor. And there wasn't anything of hers he hadn't seen or touched. At the moment she felt nothing but gratitude. "Thank you for everything."

He stared for a long moment then inclined his head in a slight nod. "They'll be taking you to a room soon."

The professional tone was reassuring. But then his eyes softened and July knew she was in trouble. "When my shift is over, I'll stop by and see how you're doing."

A knot formed in the pit of July's stomach. He remembered her. By the look in his eyes, he'd done the math.

Fear wrapped icy fingers around her neck. A.J. was always telling her she was too cynical, a glass half-empty-kind-of gal. July preferred to think of herself as a realist.

Her childhood had taught her many valuable lessons… including that men couldn't be trusted. And her encounter last summer with the smooth-talking doctor had only reinforced that belief. That's why David would never know this child was his.

A baby might not have been in her plans. She might not have instantly embraced the idea of motherhood. But now that he was here, she loved her son with her whole heart. Sharing him with a man who had no scruples simply wasn't an option.

~

David leaned back against the grey metal locker in the Jackson Hole Memorial Hospital's physician lounge. All afternoon he'd stitched lacerations, stabilized broken bones and told himself that the baby boy he'd delivered at 11:28 this morning, couldn't be his son. After all, when he and July had spent the night in that hotel room in Chicago, he'd made sure they used protection-- each and every time.

However, as a physician, he knew condoms weren't one hundred percent effective. Mistakes happened. The instant the thought crossed his mind, he rejected it. That baby boy--any baby for that matter--was a miracle, not a mistake. If the child was his, he'd take responsibility.

"Why so serious? Bad day?"

"Not at all." David turned and smiled at the lanky physician with the mop of sandy-colored hair. Dr. Travis Fisher had been a good friend since high-school days. He'd been the best man at David's wedding and a pall bearer at his wife's funeral two years ago.

If there was anyone he could talk to about this awkward situation, it would be Travis. But David had never said anything about his one-night-stand with July and he didn't have time to explain it all now.

"I was just thinking that Mary Karen will have my hide if I miss one minute of Logan's birthday party," David added.

David's sister had been blessed with three little hellions, er sons. She was a great mom, but the boys were a handful and in definite need of a male influence. Unfortunately, Mary Karen's ex-husband wasn't around. He'd left Jackson last year and was now in Boston enjoying the single life he'd missed so much.

David tried to spend as much time with the boys as possible, but what the three preschoolers really needed was a dad.

David didn't see that happening, at least not any time soon. When Mary Karen wasn't caring for the boys or working as needed at the hospital, any free time was devoted to cleaning and cooking. Neither of which were particular strengths of hers.

"What's on the menu tonight?" Travis lifted a brow. "Tofu?"

David laughed. His friend was obviously thinking of the time in high school when Mary Karen had made dinner for them. "Thank God, no. Logan is on a spaghetti kick, so that's what we're having."

"It'd be hard to ruin that." Travis pointed a finger at David. "But if anyone can, my money is on your sister."

The fondness in his tone didn't surprise David. Mary Karen and Trav were old friends. They'd even dated for a short time back in high school.

"Why don't you join us?" David urged. "I'm sure she'd love to see you."

"I appreciate the offer, but duty calls." Travis gestured with one hand toward the door. "They're prepping a c-section for me now and I have another on her way in."

"Looks like it's going to be a busy day in the nursery," David murmured, remembering how empty the beds had been over the weekend.

"Speaking of deliveries…" A speculative gleam filled Travis's hazel eyes. "I heard about your unexpected one this morning."

Travis was an OB and one of the best in town. It figured he'd heard about the delivery.

"Baby couldn't wait for you to show up." David kept his tone offhand. "He has a good set of lungs on him. Cute little fella."

"The mother's pretty easy on the eyes, too." Travis wiggled his brows. It was a skill David hadn't seen in years. "According to her admission form, she's single. I stopped and saw her before I came down here. You don't see eyes that shade of green all that often."

"I didn't notice her eyes," David said pointedly. "I didn't have time because I was too busy doing your work."

"Ouch." Travis brought a hand to his chest and stumbled back against the locker in a melodramatic gesture. "Felt that one."

David just chuckled.

But when Travis straightened, his gaze grew sharp and assessing. "A man would have to be blind not to notice those eyes."

An intern who'd been helping out in the emergency room earlier, exited the lavatory and cast a curious glance their way.

"She had good prenatal care." Travis acknowledged the other doctor with a nod while effortlessly changing the direction of the conversation.

"I'm sure the Sun Times has good insurance," David responded then cursed himself when Travis paused, head cocked.

"She told me she's a freelance photographer." Travis spoke slowly and David could almost see the mental wheels spinning. "She didn't say anything about working for a newspaper."

"I must have misunderstood." David grabbed his jacket. "Gotta go. I want to check on her and the baby before I head over to Mary Karen's house."

"No need." Travis waved a dismissive hand. "I already looked in on her. And John Watson is following the baby."

"It's not a bother." David kept his tone casual. "I don't get to deliver many babies. I want to make sure everything is okay."

Travis arched a brow. "Are you sure that's all it is?"

The guy was like a dog with a bone. David exhaled harshly and raked a hand through his hair. Maybe he should just tell Travis the whole story. Before he could yield to the impulse, the alarm on his watch buzzed. No time for confessions today. He slammed his locker shut and strode to the front door. "I really have to go."

"What am I going to tell the nurses?" Travis hurried to catch up. "You didn't give me squat."

"What are you talking about?" David didn't break stride.

"I'm not naming names, but the day shift told me you couldn't keep your eyes off the new mommy. They got the impression you knew her and asked me to get the inside scoop."

David skidded to a stop on the shiny linoleum, keeping a firm grip on his temper. Hospital gossip drove him crazy but he'd long ago learned the best way to handle it. "Tell them the new mommy and I have been having a torrid affair and I'm madly in love with her. Oh, and you can tell them that the baby is mine, too."

As he expected, Travis chuckled.

"I'll let 'em know it's a false alarm." He clapped David on the back. "Enjoy the party and give that pretty sister of yours a kiss for me."

"If you want to kiss her," David shot back, "you're going to have to do that yourself."

But as David left the lounge, he found his mind not on his sister or his nephew's party. It was on the woman upstairs in room 202. And on the baby in the nursery. The boy with the dark wavy hair…just like his own.

CHAPTER TWO

In an attempt to avoid elevator small talk, David took the stairs to the second floor. Once he reached the nurse's station, he chatted with the staff while flipping through July's thin chart. There wasn't much information. She'd listed her marital status as single, her job as a freelance photographer and her address as Chicago, Illinois. There was no next of kin listed, so if she was involved with someone, the relationship couldn't be that significant.

He wondered what had happened to her job at the Sun-Times and what had brought her to Jackson. While this was a beautiful part of the country and he was proud to call it home, it wasn't a "passing through" kind of place.

Well, he'd find out soon enough. David squared his shoulders and with clipboard in hand, turned and headed down the hall with purposeful strides. Only when he reached her room did he hesitate. Travis *was* following her now so there was really no reason for him to see her. Except he'd delivered her baby and they were old friends...of sorts.

Feeling as awkward as a fifteen-year-old, David rapped lightly on the partially closed door then pushed it open.

July sat in the bed with a tray of food before her, dressed in a simple hospital gown. She wasn't show-stopping pretty, not like Celeste, but there was something about her that was compelling. Though she couldn't be more than five foot three, with her big green eyes, shoulder length auburn hair and a creamy complexion, she'd stand out in any crowd.

If she was surprised to see him, it didn't show. She placed the dish of orange gelatin on the tray and stared at the red stitching on his lab coat. "I thought your name was spelled W-A-L-L."

Relief washed over him. She remembered his name...even if she was off on the spelling. In the delivery room he hadn't been sure she'd recognized him. And he hadn't known how to ask.

"Because it's pronounced the same, lots of people get the spelling wrong." He ambled to the bed, hoping the tension which held him in a stranglehold didn't show. "What's this I hear? The nurses tell me you haven't even been here twenty-four hours and you're already asking when you can leave."

"My insurance policy has a high deductible." She lifted her chin. "I'm a cost-conscious consumer."

David rocked back on his heels and cursed his insensitivity. The comment had been meant to tease, to break the ice, not make her feel bad. "If you need financial assistance, we have a wonderful social service department. I can have someone stop—"

"You misunderstand," she interrupted. "I have savings. I just want to keep as much of it as possible."

"Of course. Excellent. Well, if you change your mind, let me know." David found himself stumbling over the words. Normally he could talk to anyone about anything. Yet here he stood, tongue-tied and awkward. Feeling this unsure didn't make any sense. Neither did her coolness. They'd parted on good terms.

"Barring anything unforeseen, you should be able to go home tomorrow," he said finally when the silence grew intolerable. "One of our home health nurses will check on you twenty-four hours after you leave the hospital. It's an extra service we offer."

July's emerald eyes took on a distant look. "I'll need to buy a car seat and then come back for Adam—"

"When you leave here you need to take it easy," he said in a firm voice, as if she were one of his patients. "The baby will be staying with us for a while longer so there's no rush on the car seat."

"The nurses told me he was doing fine." Fear skittered across her face and her eyes filled with tears. "Has something happened to him?"

"He's a little jaundiced. Not unexpected in a premi." David spoke in what he hoped was a reassuring tone. Though he didn't have a lot to do with obstetrics, the hormone surge experienced after delivery was well-documented. He should have chosen his words more carefully.

"When my water broke, I knew it was too early." Her voice cracked and she collapsed back against the pillows, looking much younger than her twenty-six years. "I couldn't stop it. Everything went so fast…"

"There wasn't anything you could have done differently." He resisted the urge to pat her on the shoulder. "Your body was ready to deliver when you walked through the door."

"I don't know how that happened," July continued, almost to herself. "The doctor swore I'd go late."

"What was your due date?" David asked in as casual a tone as he could muster.

"April 15th."

The tension which had been gripping his shoulders slid to his chest. He'd been calculating dates in his mind from the moment he'd recognized her name on the medical record and had seen her swollen belly. If she was due the middle of April she'd have gotten pregnant around the time they'd been together in Chicago. Though he thought he was doing a good job at keeping his emotions from his face, he knew he'd failed when her gaze narrowed.

"Don't worry." She waved a hand. "He's not your baby."

"How can you be sure he's not mine?" The second the question shot from his lips David wondered if he'd lost his mind. She'd just handed him a free pass and he was arguing? But a man didn't walk away from his responsibilities. "The dates match."

"We used a condom," she reminded him. "*Every* time."

"Are you telling me you had unprotected sex with someone else around that time?"

"Look." She shoved the tray table out of the way and leaned forward. "The Sir Galahad act is unnecessary. Adam is not your son."

She sounded sincere. What she said made sense. But he remembered that night as if it were yesterday. There had been nothing practiced in her responses, which told him she hadn't been with a man in a while. Now she expected him to believe she'd spent the night with him then promptly went out and had sex with another guy? It was possible, but his gut told him she was lying.

He didn't like doubting her. She'd impressed him from the onset as being one of those people who told it as she saw it. He'd liked that about her.

David opened his mouth to ask one of half a dozen questions poised on the tip of his tongue, but shut it without speaking. The set of her jaw told him he wasn't going to get anything more from her. At least not by going the direct route.

He rocked back on his heels. "Are you really going to call him Adam?"

"What's wrong with it?"

David hid a smile at the challenge in her tone. Feisty. That was another of the qualities that had drawn him to her in that hotel bar. "When I was a boy, our next-door neighbors had two bulldogs. One named Adam. The other, Eve."

"Well, I have a good friend named Adam and he's definitely not a dog."

A good friend? By the caring in her tone...definitely. But more? David fought an unexpected surge of jealousy, before remembering she hadn't even given this guy's name as an emergency contact. "How'd you meet? Neighbors?"

July lifted a shoulder in an unconcerned shrug. "Foster care."

Just when he thought he was beginning to get a handle on her, she'd surprised him again. Without waiting for an invitation, David dropped to sit on the edge of her bed. "You never told me you grew up in foster care."

"If you remember, once we got to your room that night, we didn't do much talking."

David thought back. She was right. Once that hotel door had clicked shut and they'd hit the bed there hadn't been much conversation. Lots of moaning but not much intelligible communication. But had she forgotten how they'd sat in the hotel bar for hours doing nothing but talking?

"We discussed all sorts of things before that," David insisted. "Triathlon training. Best Indie Horror movies. Food favorites."

"We talked about our likes and dislikes," July reminded him. "But we shared very little about our personal lives."

He paused for a moment and realized she was right. She hadn't mentioned anything about her childhood. He hadn't mentioned he'd had a wife who'd died. "Foster care couldn't have been easy."

An unreadable look filled her eyes. "What doesn't kill us makes us stronger."

Those horrible days after the car accident flashed before him. Though David didn't feel stronger, at least he no longer dwelled on something that couldn't be changed. "I'm surprised you weren't adopted."

Instead of a quick comeback, she paused, her green eyes dark. "It was...complicated."

"Tell me," he urged when she didn't continue.

She shook her head. When the bull-dog set to her jaw returned he knew she'd shared all she was going to on the matter.

"How did you end up here anyway?" Her gaze narrowed. "When we met, you were supposedly living in Minneapolis and planning to move to Chicago."

"No supposedly about it. I was working at Hennepin but had accepted the position at Rush when you and I talked." David shifted his gaze out the window and let it linger on the snowy mountain peaks in the distance.

He'd felt so lost after Celeste's death. So alone. Unable to shake the sadness, he'd moved to the Twin Cities, hoping a change of scene would help. It hadn't. He'd been planning another move, this time to Chicago, the night he'd met July.

"What happened?" she asked.

"I had lunch with an old friend the day after we were together. We'd known each other a long time. He knew my—" David paused, "—situation. After talking to him I realized that being in Jackson—with my family—was where I belonged."

"Please, don't let me keep you from your *family*," she said, her green eyes as cool as her tone.

"I still have a few minutes." David needed to get to his nephew's party but just like the last time they were together, he found himself reluctant to leave her. "How did your friend Adam respond when you called and gave him the good news?"

"I haven't been able to reach him," she said in a matter-of-fact tone.

The announcement over the PA system advised visitors it was time to leave. David glanced at the clock on the wall. Ten minutes to get to his sister's house. Ten minutes or he was in the dog-house for life. He rose to his feet. "I'd better go."

She didn't say another word, merely gave him a polite smile, the kind you'd give a casual acquaintance you didn't plan to see again.

"I'll check on you tomorrow," he promised even as he edged

closer to the door, still reluctant to leave. "See how you're feeling, make sure you're up to going home."

"There's no need—"

The door swung open and an older staff nurse who'd worked for the hospital since David had been a baby, stepped into the room, a blue-wrapped bundle in her arms. "Mrs. Greer, you have a visitor."

David saw July flinch at the "Mrs." but she didn't correct the woman. Instead her full attention was now on the baby.

The grey-haired woman stopped when she saw David. "Dr. Wahl. I didn't mean to interrupt. I didn't realize you were still here."

"It's fine. I was on my way out." David knew his sister and family were waiting. Knew his nephews would refuse to start the party until he got there. Even so, he took an extra second to linger and admire the baby that very easily could be his.

~

"Thanks for coming tonight." Mary Karen Vaughn stood beside David on the porch of the large two-story white clapboard she shared with her three sons, her maternal grandmother, Fern, and super-sized cockapoo, Henry. "Logan was so excited to see you."

"Three little boys throwing cake at each other." David winked. "Wouldn't have missed it for the world."

Actually, during the evening the terrible trio had been fairly well-behaved. And the war-whoop the twins and Logan had let loose when he'd walked through the door had warmed his heart. Of course, with his parents on a European cruise, his only competition was Granny Fern. While the boys loved their great-grandmother, they'd stuck tight to his side all evening.

After spaghetti had been eaten and two candles blown out on the cake, Granny had gone to her room for some well-needed "shut-eye." Last week she'd tripped over the dog and cracked a rib.

Though Granny loved helping with the boys and watching them while Mary Karen worked an occasional shift at the hospital, David worried about her. The older woman needed more rest than she was able to get in this busy household.

That was one of the reasons he'd stayed and helped Mary Karen get the boys bathed and in bed. But that wasn't the only reason. Keeping busy kept thoughts of July at bay.

"You're so good with the boys." Mary Karen turned to the rail and stared out into the darkness. Far off in the distance, a coyote wailed. She pulled her coat tight around her. "You and Celeste should have had children."

Celeste had liked Mary Karen as much as she'd liked anyone in Jackson, but David knew his sister had hoped more closeness would come when they had children in common.

David wasn't sure it would have made a difference. Celeste had been so different from his down-to-earth sister. Different than most of the women in Jackson. He smiled. His wife had been a hot-house rose in a sea of wildflowers.

It wasn't an exaggeration to say Celeste had been the most beautiful woman in Jackson. Men would stop on the street and stare when she walked by. She'd been a city girl to the core, a woman who'd loved shopping, travel and him. When they'd left California and moved to Jackson, she'd kept her job as a marketing rep for a company based in Los Angeles. He'd worried about her being on the road so much, but accepted the fact that she loved her job too much to quit.

Then two years ago, on her way to the airport for a business trip, her sports car had been broadsided by a drunk driver. She'd been killed instantly. When he'd heard the news, a part of him had died with her.

At the time Mary Karen had just delivered Logan. Connor and Caleb, the twins, had just turned two. While his sister's household had always been chaotic, to add to her stress, her husband of three years had started making noises like he'd rather be single.

"I wish we'd had a baby, too," David murmured into the quiet stillness. "But we wanted to wait for just the right moment. We thought we had all the time in the world."

The darkness surrounding them made it easier to speak of the past.

"I think we've both learned there are no guarantees. Life can be going along just fine then poof...everything changes." The pain in her voice made David long to slam a fist into his ex-brother-in-law's face.

"You're right." David reached down absently scratched the head of Henry, the large cockapoo standing beside him.

"Change isn't always bad," Mary Karen said, her optimistic nature shining above the gloom. "It can be good. Unexpected doesn't always mean unwanted."

David thought of the woman in the maternity wing and the baby boy who slumbered in the nursery. His baby? Or the child of another man?

He hadn't planned on being a father, but if that child was his, he wouldn't walk away. Like his sister said...just because something is unexpected, didn't mean it's unwanted.

CHAPTER THREE

July pulled on her maternity jeans and slipped a dark green cotton shirt over her head. Although she'd gained only twenty pounds with this pregnancy—and had lost a good chunk of it yesterday--she wasn't quite ready for skinny jeans and a fitted sweater. Thankfully most of the simple styles she'd purchased while pregnant didn't have a "maternity" look.

Dealing with clothes was the least of her concerns. Where to go once she and Adam returned to Chicago, now that had her worried. Before she'd started on her four-national-parks-in–four-months photo shoot, her home had been the basement of a friend from her newspaper days. A woman who'd made it clear she could live there only until the baby arrived. Apparently, the husband had a strong aversion to crying infants.

A.J. had told her she could room with him once his roommate moved out May 1. That date would have been perfect if the baby had come late as the doctor predicted.

When a door slams shut it means God is pointing to an open door further on down.

The verse had been on a needle-point pillow at the home

where she'd stayed when her mom had been in rehab for the third time. The mother in that family had been a needlepoint fanatic who never met a saying she didn't want to stitch.

July took a deep breath and let it out slowly. Everything would work out. She'd made good money photographing wildlife in some of the most beautiful national parks in the United States. Yellowstone had been the final one on the list and she'd finished shooting less than forty-eight hours earlier.

Nylah, the woman who was her liaison with Outdoor Life magazine, had gushed over the images.

A sense of satisfaction rose inside July. When she'd lost her job at the newspaper due to cutbacks, she'd been devastated. The loss had turned out to be an unexpected blessing.

Photographing nature had always been her passion. Whether it was a single flower growing out of a crack in the concrete or an imposing Bighorn on a rocky ledge, she was happiest outdoors with a camera in her hand.

The tension in her shoulders had begun to ease when the cell phone in her pocket buzzed. July pulled it out and glanced at the readout. *Nylah.* Her heart picked up speed. Hopefully the woman was calling to tell her the magazine had approved the Yellowstone shots.

Moving slowly to the door, July closed it all the way before hitting the talk button. "Hello, Nylah."

"Ohmygod, I can't believe it's finally you. I was starting to think you'd been abducted by aliens." The words ran together, tumbling out one after the other. "I've been calling the motel since last night. When I finally reached the guy at the front desk, I panicked when he told me he hadn't seen you since yesterday morning. He told me to call your cell, but it kept going straight to voice mail."

"I forgot to charge it." A sick feeling rolled around in the pit of July's stomach. While Nylah had loved the photos, July knew

final approval would come from someone at Outdoor Life magazine. "Is this about the photos? Is something wrong? If they want
me to reshoot—"

"No, this isn't about them. The photos were marvelous. Love
them. Love them. Love them." Nylah paused. "Now that I think
about it, the reason I'm calling does involve the pictures, but only
in the very best of ways."

Now thoroughly confused, July took a seat on the edge of the
bed. "So Outdoor Life approved the Yellowstone photos?"

"Yes, Yes, but that's not why we need to talk. Are you ready?"

July rolled her eyes and reclined against the pillow, the phone
resting against her ear. "Ready."

"Were you aware that I had several other photographers in
Yellowstone taking pictures of the Bighorns?"

"No." July's fingers tightened around the phone. The elderly
guide had said something about bringing other "shutter-bugs" to
several of the sites where she'd gone. At the time she'd assumed
he was talking about tourists, not other photographers.

"It was a competition of sorts." Nylah's voice rose. "You won."

July loosened her death grip on the phone. "I did?"

"Absolutely. A well-known writer recently contacted me. He
has a contract to do a series of books on wildlife in America.
After checking out the Bighorn shots from everyone, he selected
you to take the photos from this part of the country. If he likes
what he sees even half as much as the Bighorn Sheep, he may ask
for more," Nylah said. "He's willing to pay—"

The amount Nylah mentioned made July gasp. As the woman
continued to talk, July realized this meant she'd have to remain in
Jackson for at least another month. While that probably wasn't
the wisest thing to do--with David and his family living here--
the money was too good to turn down.

"Can you start today?" Nylah asked.

"Uh, today's not good." July had heard stories of women who

had babies in the field and continued to work. Call her a wimp but she needed some time to recharge before tackling mountain trails. "How about next week?"

That would give her time to bring the baby home and get settled. Dr. Fisher had said she could resume light activity in a week.

"That will be okay, I suppose." Nylah didn't sound exactly thrilled about the delay but then with her, everything was business. "Is it the pregnancy? I know you're due soon--"

"I had the baby yesterday." Though she tried to be matter-of-fact, July heard the lilt in her voice. That wasn't surprising considering that every time she thought about her beautiful son she couldn't help but smile.

"Wonderful news," Nylah said. "I was concerned this whole giving-birth-thing might interfere but it sounds like you've got it under control."

"Thank you," July said before she realized Nylah hadn't congratulated her, not really.

"Knowing what a resourceful young woman you are, I'm sure you have childcare all arranged."

"Childcare?" July said in a voice that seemed to come from far away.

"Surely you didn't plan on taking the baby with you."

"Um. No. Of course not," July murmured even as her mind raced. Until this moment she hadn't even considered that she'd have to find someone to care for her tiny baby. Still, if she wanted a roof over her head and food to eat, she had to keep working.

"Good." Though Nylah had projected complete confidence up to this point, July heard the relief in her voice. "And congrats again. I don't need to tell you this is a great coup. The other photographers had more impressive portfolios, but the photos you took were clearly the best."

"Ms. Greer. Is this a bad time?"

July glanced at the dark-haired young woman standing in the doorway with a hospital name tag. Her stylish linen dress in pale yellow was the perfect foil for her dark hair. Not only did she have beautiful features but her make-up had obviously been applied with a deft touch, making her amber eyes look large and luminous.

"Nylah, I need to run. Call you later." July clicked off the phone and placed it on the tray table.

"You didn't need to do that," the woman demurred. "I could have come back."

"That's okay." July slid the phone into her pocket. "We were through talking anyway."

"I'm Lexi Brennan." The woman crossed the room and held out her hand. "I'm a social worker at Jackson Hole Memorial and part of our discharge planning team."

July forced a smile. While this woman seemed nice, social workers had been the enemy during most of her childhood. They lived their life by the book, forced to follow guidelines even when those regulations meant returning a little girl over and over again to her addict mother.

Lexi gestured with one hand to the chair by the bed. "Mind if I sit for a moment?"

"Please, do." July swung her legs over the side of the bed, her curiosity aroused. Was the woman here because of the hospital bill or concern over Adam's well-being?

Stop, July told herself. *You are a decent, law-abiding citizen. There is no reason to worry.* Still, fear bubbled up inside her. "What is it you want?"

The thought burst from her lips; the tone impertinent, bordering on rude. July wasn't sure who was more surprised, the social worker or herself.

July froze. Her heart slammed against her ribs. She opened her mouth but shut it without speaking.

To her surprise, Lexi chuckled. "I like someone who gets right to the heart of the matter."

The social worker's graciousness made July feel even worse.

"I stopped to see if you needed any help with your post-hospital plans." Lexi glanced down at the chart in her hand. "I noticed you listed your home address as Chicago. Will you be returning there once your baby is discharged?"

Before July could answer, a loud buzzing sounded from the pager clipped to the waistband of Lexi's skirt. The social worker dropped her gaze to the readout then her brows furrowed. "I apologize. The family of a patient in our ICU has arrived. I really need to speak with them. Would it be okay if I came back in say...a half hour?"

July wished she could tell her she didn't need to bother returning, that she had it all under control. But that would be a lie. She needed to find a place to live and someone to watch Adam. The social worker appeared to be her best resource.

"Will that work for you?" Lexi asked again, glancing toward the door.

"Absolutely." July injected some enthusiasm into her voice. Lexi had been so gracious. She deserved the same consideration in return. "Dr. Fisher still needs to stop by before I can be released. The nurses don't expect him for another hour or so."

"Thanks for being so understanding." Lexi had almost reached the door by the time she finished speaking. "I'll be back as soon as possible."

After the social worker left, July snagged her purse from the bedside stand. She'd showered this morning but hadn't done much else. Lexi was so pretty, so put together that July couldn't help but feel dowdy beside her.

Pulling a tube of mascara from her bag, July added some length to her lashes then shifted her attention on her mouth. With a quick flick she dipped her finger into a pot o'gloss and pressed some color to her lips. Once that was applied to her satisfaction, she found a tiny tube of travel gel and took a couple minutes to tame a few wayward stands of hair. She smiled at herself in the compact. Much, much better.

"You look as if you're feeling better this morning." A familiar deep voice sounded from the doorway.

July groaned. She'd hoped to be gone before David's shift ended. No such luck. She snapped the compact closed, dropped it into her bag and shifted to face him. "I thought you'd be working."

Or home with your wife. Bitterness rose inside her at his duplicity. What made her the angriest was that she'd asked his marital status shortly after he'd began flirting with her in the hotel bar. Only after she found out she was pregnant with his baby and tried to track him down did she discover that he'd lied. According to a former colleague, the handsome young doctor who'd swept her off her feet wasn't single. Dr. David Wahl had a "gorgeous" wife at home.

"I don't go in today until three." He pulled the door closed. Instead of a white jacket he wore khakis and a royal blue polo that made his eyes look bluer than the sky outside her window. "I came to see if you'd like to have lunch with me in the hospital cafeteria. The food is edible and it'll give us a chance to catch up."

Catch up? What was there to catch up on? Unless he meant to confess that he had a wife he'd forgotten to mention, which she highly doubted. "With that ringing endorsement, it'd be hard to say no."

"You'll join me?"

His delighted smile was almost her undoing. The same electricity that had been there eight months ago sizzled in the room. This time she ignored it. She didn't want anything to do with a cheater.

"I'm being dismissed." She glanced at her watch. "Once Dr. Fisher stops by, I'll be on my way."

"What about your boyfriend, er I mean your friend?" he asked, his gaze watchful. "Did you ever reach him?"

"I did. He'd been out celebrating. He landed a role in a Broadway touring company," July kept her tone even. "He'd just gotten off the phone with his agent finalizing the details when we connected."

"Was he excited about the baby?"

"*Very* excited." July forced some enthusiasm into her voice. A.J. had actually been more jazzed about his new role than her new son. But that was understandable. The theater was his life now. He'd been around too many kids growing up to be excited about one more, even if that one was hers.

"When is he coming?"

"He's not." July brushed a piece of lint from her jeans. "The tour starts in two weeks. A.J. was a last-minute replacement, so he's got lots of catching up to do."

July understood how important this was to him, truly she did. This was his big break. Still, she couldn't help but wish he'd been a little more excited for her.

The look on David's face said he didn't understand either. Instead of consoling her, it made July wish she'd kept her mouth shut or made something up. The less David knew about her personal life, the better.

"How long will you be staying in Jackson?" David asked in a tone so casual it sent red flags popping up.

"I'm not sure," she hedged.

July couldn't figure out why he kept coming around. If she were him, she'd be keeping her distance. This wasn't a big impersonal town like Chicago. Jackson was small and everyone knew people in small towns loved to gossip. If David wasn't careful, someone was going to mention his intense interest in her and her baby to his wife.

"Before Adam leaves the hospital, I'd like to have a test done on him. But I need your permission."

July pulled her brows together. "If you're talking about the testing for PKU and the others they recommend for newborns, I had no problem with them."

"I'm not talking about those tests."

"What then?"

"A paternity test." His blue eyes locked on hers. "I need to know if Adam is mine."

CHAPTER FOUR

When July was five her mother had shoved her against a wall so hard it pushed all the air from her lungs. She remembered that horrible, scary feeling. She felt the same way now.

But July was no stranger to having her life take an ugly turn. She forced herself to breathe normally. "I already told you he isn't yours. Most men would be jumping for joy at that news."

"I'm not most men." His gaze never left her face. "If Adam is my son, I want to be a part of his life. I want him to know me. I want to be his dad."

The sincerity in his tone touched the part of July's heart that had once yearned for a father's love. The part which had hoped her dad—whoever he was—would one day show up and rescue her from the misery that was her childhood.

She reminded herself they weren't talking about her. They were talking about Adam. And she wasn't her mother. Her child would always have her love and support.

"July." David's voice, soft but insistent, broke through her reverie. "Will you consent to the test?"

She curbed her irritation at his persistence. It was obvious, at least to her, that he hadn't thought this through. "First I'd like to ask you a question."

"Sure." He dropped into the chair next to the bed. "Ask me anything."

"Why are you determined to go ahead with this? I've already told you—assured you—that Adam isn't your son." July kept her tone even, though she was shaking clear down to her bare toes. "If it's done—for really no good reason—your wife will likely find out. Is that what you really want?"

She'd presented the facts in a calm manner. Still, she waited for the explosion. Growing up, she'd learned what can happen when you questioned someone's decision. This time, all she got was a puzzled look.

"What are you talking about? I'm not married."

July let out the breath she'd been holding. Oh, he was good. If she didn't know the truth, she'd find his protest completely believable. While he may have fooled her once, it wasn't going to happen again.

"There's no need to continue with the game." Again, July kept her anger at being deceived under tight wraps and spoke in a matter-of-fact tone. "Remember the doctor who stopped by the table the night we first met? The one my reporter friend knew?"

David's gaze turned thoughtful. He nodded. "Kevin Countryman."

"That's the one. Well, my friend ran into him a couple months later." When July discovered she was pregnant, she'd called hospitals in Minneapolis and in Chicago looking for Dr. David Wall. Of course, because of spelling his name wrong, she'd never found him. Then she'd remembered Dr. Countryman. She'd asked her friend to contact him in the hopes he'd know where to find David.

"And—" David prompted.

"During the course of their conversation he mentioned you

were married." July had been overwhelmed with a deep sense of betrayal. That same day she'd abandoned her search.

"Wait a minute. You've got it all wr—"

"He said your wife was gorgeous, like a model. He told my friend he'd been surprised to see you flirting with me." The words had been a knife to her heart. Saying them brought the pain flooding back. Okay, so maybe she wasn't America's Next Top Model, but she'd been told many, many times that she was "cute" and had beautiful eyes.

"July. Listen to me."

"All I'm asking is that you think of your wife's feelings." She maintained an even tone. Goodness knows, she'd had a lifetime of practice. "I want you to realize that if news of the DNA test gets out, she will be hurt by the scandal. And all for nothing because Adam is not your son."

Some of the light in his eyes dimmed at her words. It was almost as if he wanted Adam to be his. Which was insane. What married man would welcome a baby from a one-night-stand?

"We need to clear one thing up right now," David said in a firm voice. "I.am.not.married."

When she opened her mouth to protest, he held up a hand.

"Please let me finish. I was married. My wife died the year before you and I met." His gaze met hers. "I'd never have slept with you if I'd been married. For Celeste and me, those marriage vows were sacred."

July's head spun like an out-of-control tilt-a-whirl. Everything from David's body posture to his facial expression to his intonation said he was telling the truth. Yet she had a reliable third party with no stakes in the matter who said differently.

"Dr. Countryman knew you," she finally managed to sputter. "How could he not have known your wife had died?"

"I knew Kevin back in residency." David's eyes never left hers. "It's been a long time since I've spoken to him. Celeste must have been still alive the last time we talked."

"I don't know. That seems—"

"You still don't believe me." David rose and paced the room, frustration written all over his face. "Ask anyone. Ask Lexi or Dr. Fisher. They'll confirm that what I've told you is true."

A cold chill stole over July. Relief that she hadn't slept with a married man was miniscule compared to the stark realization that the tables had turned. She was now the one who needed to apologize. She'd told David to his face that Adam wasn't his son. Not once. Many times.

Tell him you're sorry. Tell him you made a mistake. He'll understand. You thought he was married...

July opened her mouth but the words wouldn't come. Her heart pounded hard and fast in her head making it impossible for her to think, much less form a coherent sentence.

"July," David's voice, soft but insistent, broke through the maelstrom in her head. "Will you consent to the test?"

She tried to speak but settled for a jerky nod.

"The test is easy." Though his tone was professional, she could hear the undercurrent of relief in his voice. "A simple buccal swab. One to Adam's cheek, one to yours."

"Mine?" Her voice broke on the word.

"It's recommended," he said quickly. "If you don't want—"

"No problem." July took a glass of water from the tray-table and chugged it past her dry throat. "Just give me a call when—-"

"We can do it now." He pulled two vials from his pocket along with an official looking paper. "First I need your signature."

The room closed around her neck like a noose. She took the paper from his hand and sweat trickled down her back. "Once we do this, how long before you get the results?"

"Three to five days."

The noose tightened.

July pretended to study the consent form but the words blurred. After a moment, she folded the paper in half and dropped it into her purse.

"What are you doing?" Confusion blanketed his face. "You said you'd do it."

Though her heart now beat like a trapped butterfly in her chest, she somehow managed a nonchalant air. "I'm sure you understand me wanting to thoroughly read a legal document. I'll be in Jackson Hole for at least another month. We'll definitely do the test before I leave."

"Why wait so long?" His brows pulled together. "It doesn't take a month to read the authorization."

"Because I know what the answer will be, and I'm in no hurry." *Because I need to tell you the truth before you get the results.*

"You'll have it done before you leave."

"Absolutely." July wished she could bring herself to tell him the test wasn't needed. After all, he was the only one she'd been with in over three years. But every time she tried to bring the words forth, tentacles of fear slipped around her, squeezing out the air.

She would tell David. In her own time. In her own way. Telling him had to be done soon. Before the DNA test. Before he became even more suspicious. Before he found out the truth on his own...

David left July's room, feeling more unsettled than when he'd walked through the door. Last night, while tossing and turning in bed he'd considered his options. He could take July at her word that Adam wasn't his son. But if she was lying, once she left Jackson Hole, she'd be taking his flesh-and-blood out of his life forever. Or he could be proactive and find out for sure if that baby in the nursery was his.

He'd told himself her response to his request for a DNA test would tell him a lot. If she refused, it'd confirm his suspicions that she was lying. She hadn't refused. At least not directly.

"Can I help you, doctor?"

David looked into the eyes of Madi Oliver, the emergency room nurse who'd been at July's side during the delivery. He glanced around the nursery. "What are you doing here? This isn't the ER."

"Very perceptive." Madi smiled. "It was slow downstairs so they sent me up here to help out."

He didn't know Madi all that well. David only knew she was an excellent nurse and good with the patients.

"What brings you to the nursery?"

David glanced around. He hadn't consciously planned to make a detour to this part of the hospital but now that he was here, he might as well assuage his curiosity. "I stopped by to check on the Greer baby."

"Of course." Madi smiled and he suddenly realized with her dark hair and big blue eyes she was quite pretty. It didn't matter. There was no sizzle. Not like there was with July...

While she was retrieving the baby, David scrubbed his hands and put on a gown, wondering why he insisted on tormenting himself. For all he knew this little boy was someone else's son.

"Here he is."

David held out his arms and Madi placed the baby in them. Wrapped securely in a blue blanket and wearing a cap of the same color, the infant didn't cry, just stared at him with serious eyes.

The rush of emotion took David by surprise as did the powerful connection he felt to this tiny baby. He tightened his arms protectively around the child he'd brought into the world barely twenty-four hours earlier. "He's so light."

"He's small," Madi agreed, "but doing really well. Once we get his bilirubin down a bit more, he'll be able to go home."

Dave gazed at the tiny face, searching for a family resemblance. Other than the dark hair—now covered—the baby could belong to anyone.

"I only wish the Simpson baby was doing as well." Although they were alone in this part of the nursery, Madi spoke in a low tone. "It looks like she'll have to go home with the feeding tube. Kayla started crying this morning when the doctor told her."

David had grown up with Kayla Simpson and her husband. Their long-awaited pregnancy had been trouble-free but their little girl had been born with several congenital anomalies. "Has Lexi been up to talk with them?"

Since joining the hospital staff five years ago, the social worker had proven to be a valuable member of the hospital team.

"She'll be here once she's done in the ICU." A look of sadness swept across the RN's face. "She's talking to the Evans family about organ donation."

The six months David had spent at Hennepin in Minneapolis had made him appreciate just how different it was to practice emergency medicine at a large trauma center versus a community hospital like this one. Here, other than tourists, most of the people he treated were ones he knew. Tim Evans, a gregarious high school baseball coach, belonged to his church. The guy had taken a turn too fast on his cycle and had cracked his unhelmeted head on the concrete.

"A life ends." David dropped his gaze to the baby and stroked the soft cheek with his finger. "Another begins."

When he looked up and saw the pain in Madi's eyes, he realized the simple observation may have opened an old wound. Before he could say another word, Madi's expression cleared and she lifted a hand in greeting. "Here's Lexi now."

David shifted his gaze to the social worker. Her smile never wavered, but her eyes filled with curiosity at the sight of the blue bundle in his arms.

Resisting the urge to shove the baby back into Madi's care, he met the social worker's smile with one of his own.

"Madi mentioned the Simpson baby is going home with a feeding tube," he said in lieu of a greeting. "Sounds like Kayla is taking the news hard."

"This has been such a shock for both of them," Lexi agreed. "Kayla is a strong woman. She and John will weather this crisis. I'll make sure they have the support they need."

David nodded then casually handed the baby back to Madi. "I have to get going."

Lexi took a step forward and peered at the baby. "Who's this little guy?"

"This is Adam Greer," Madi explained. "Our emergency room baby."

"I thought Dr. Watson was following him?"

"He is," David said, trying not to get defensive. After all, it was a logical question. "I don't get a chance to deliver many babies, so this one is sort of special."

Lexi lifted a brow. "How's he doing?"

"Jaundiced, but he should be able to be released in a day or so," David said.

"I wonder where he'll go home to," Madi mused.

"What do you mean?" Lexi asked.

David's ears pricked up.

"His mother had been living in the motel across the street from the Community Playhouse before she delivered," Madi informed Lexi. "Hardly a suitable environment for a baby."

"I agree with you." Lexi glanced down at her clipboard. "I'll add post-discharge housing to my discussion list. After I finish here, I'm headed to her room."

CHAPTER FIVE

July stared at the birth certificate application that had been left for her to fill out. She'd been told she had to complete and turn it in before she was dismissed.

The section asking for her information had been easy. The field for the baby's name was completed without hesitation. She'd had almost five months—since she'd first learned she was carrying a boy—to decide on his name. It was the section asking for the father's information that stopped her cold.

How could she put David's name on the application before she'd told him Adam was his son? Still, she couldn't bring herself to write the word that had been on her own birth certificate.

She'd found hers stuffed in the back of a drawer the summer she turned thirteen. Though her mother had always maintained her father could have been any one of a number of men, July had thought she was exaggerating. It wasn't until she'd seen "unknown" on that birth certificate that her dreams of a father one day appearing on a white horse to rescue her had disappeared in a puff of smoke.

July took a deep breath then let it out slowly. She picked up the pen, still unsure. Unlike her mother, there was no doubt in

July's mind about Adam's father. But what if David got hold of the certificate? Or some staff member noticed his name on the application and mentioned it to him?

The form was still incomplete when the door creaked open and Lexi stuck her face in the room. "Can I come in?"

"Certainly." This time July offered a welcoming smile to the social worker.

"I'm sorry about the delay." The brunette's heels clacked loudly on the shiny linoleum as she hurried across the room. "I didn't think I'd be so long."

"No worries." July dropped the pen, thankful for the diversion. "I'm still waiting for Dr. Fisher to stop by and release me."

"What are you working on?" Lexi asked.

"The birth certificate application," July said, trying not to sigh.

Lexi's gaze dropped to the form, taking in the part still not completed. "It can be hard to decide what to put there. At least it was for me."

"You have a child?"

"Addie is seven." Lexi's perfectly painted lips curved up in a slight smile. "It might sound corny, but she's the light of my life."

It didn't sound at all corny. Though her son was only a day old, July understood. She returned Lexi's smile.

"Does her father live in Jackson?" From a previous comment July knew the social worker wasn't married, but that didn't mean the guy wasn't in her life.

"Drew lives in Columbus, Ohio." Lexi spoke in a matter-of-fact tone. "He's not involved at all."

"Is his name on her birth certificate?" The minute the question left her lips, July wanted to call it back. Though the social worker had been forthcoming about her personal life, the question was way too personal.

"It is." Lexi took a seat in the chair by the bed with a gracefulness July envied. "I considered leaving it off. After all, once he found out I was pregnant he didn't want anything to do with me."

"Yet you put his name on her birth certificate."

"Drew is her father and him being a jerk doesn't change that." Lexi spoke matter-of-factly without a hint of emotion on her face. "Putting 'unknown' would have been a lie. I didn't want Addie's life to start off with a lie."

July leaned back against the pillow and considered the words. She'd never thought of it that way. That's what she'd be doing if she left David's name off the birth certificate.

"One of my concerns is that Adam's dad is from Jackson," July found herself admitting. "I don't want anyone knowing that he's my baby's father."

Lexi's expression turned serious. "I can assure you that the hospital places a high emphasis on maintaining confidentiality. This application will immediately go into an envelope and be mailed."

Yeah, but who puts it in the envelope?

Lexi must have sensed July still wasn't convinced because she leaned forward and placed a hand on her arm. "If you like I can take care of it myself. No one else will see it."

July cocked her head. "How about you? Will you look?"

"We're required to check the form and make sure everything is correctly completed," Lexi conceded. "I assure you that you can count on my discretion. I'd never betray a confidence."

July drew a steadying breath. She never thought she'd be faced with this decision. Of course, she'd never imagined David would be the one delivering her baby either.

"Okay." July picked up the pen. "Give me a second."

Without giving herself a chance to change her mind, July quickly completed the form. She paused for a second on David's date of birth. She knew he was thirty-two but the date escaped her. Until she remembered him saying he was born on the fourth of July.

She finished that section then handed the paper to Lexi, her palms sweaty, her pulse pounding a rat-a-tat-tat against her temples. "Could you fill in the home address for me? It should be on the hospital roster."

"The father works here?" Surprise filled Lexi's voice.

July nodded, resisting the urge to snatch the paper back. Dear God she hoped trusting Lexi wasn't a mistake.

Lexi scanned the form. July knew the instant she saw David's name because the social worker's eyes widened. She glanced up. "Dr. Wahl is your baby's father?"

"He doesn't know that Adam is his, not yet," July admitted. "He only suspects."

Lexi met her gaze. There was no condemnation in the amber eyes, not even the slightest hint of judgment. "Your reasons are your business. If you ever want to talk—"

"I won't," July said with extra firmness, making it clear the subject was closed.

Lexi slipped the form into her portfolio. "I'll get his home address then put this in the mail."

"Thank you," July said. "Before you leave, I was wondering if you have some suggestions on places to live."

July quickly filled Lexi in on her new job assignment. "My ideal location would be a place with childcare nearby. I don't want to leave Adam for any longer than necessary."

A thoughtful look crossed the social worker's face. "I know the perfect place. I have a friend who's divorced with kids of her own. Her house isn't far from downtown and she's looking for ways to bring in extra money. She might even be willing to watch Adam for you."

"That would be fabulous." July's hopes soared. The woman sounded perfect.

Lexi opened her portfolio again and scribbled a name and phone number on the back of her business card. "Give her a call. Tell her I recommended you."

July glanced down at the card. "Mary Karen Vaughn. Nice name."

"You'll love her." Lexi's lips curved in a slight smile. "Leaving Adam with Mary Karen will be like leaving him with...a favorite aunt."

~

Once July had gotten settled into her new place, she'd been exhausted and had gone to bed early. Despite overwhelming fatigue, sleep eluded her. At half past two, she gave up trying. She picked up the phone and called her oldest and dearest friend.

They talked about the baby for a few minutes and about his new gig. Then she told him about David and what she'd discovered. She could tell by the silence on the other end he was waiting for her to get down to the real reason she'd called. July took a deep breath and reminded herself this was A.J. There was nothing she couldn't say to him.

"I couldn't do it," July whispered into the phone. "All I had to do was say, 'Hey, I told you he wasn't your son because I thought you were married and I'm sorry I lied.' Super simple, right?"

"For anyone else it'd be a piece of cake," A.J. said softly. "They didn't have your life."

July had always considered herself a survivor. She and A.J. had once even officially promised each other that they would not let their past determine their future. But this latest challenge told her the past still controlled her life.

"I hate her," July said, the words hanging in the air.

"I don't blame you," A.J. spoke vehemently. "The woman wasn't fit to raise a dog."

"She locked me in a closet for spilling a bottle of booze." July's voice rose and the hand holding the phone began to shake. Her heart pounded against her ribs. "It was an accident. I told her I was sorry. I told her over and over and over again. It only seemed to make her angrier. Even when she hit me and told me to shut up, I couldn't stop saying it. Then she shoved me into that closet.

If one of her boyfriends hadn't gone looking for a coat the next day, I'd still be in there."

"I know, babe. I know."

She swiped at her tears. "I don't know why I'm going on and on. You've heard it all before. Besides it was a long time ago anyway."

"It may have been a long time ago, but those kinds of memories stick with you."

"I've tried to put them in the past. Take those horrible memories and stuff them in some sort of mental box and throw away the key. That hasn't worked." July expelled a frustrated breath. "Every time I even think of telling David I'm sorry I lied to him, it's like I'm back in that closet, hearing her scream at me to shut up."

"July." A.J. paused for a long moment. "You know I'm not big on shrinks…"

"You think I'm crazy, don't you? You think--"

"I think you're very strong. I think you wouldn't have made it through all you've had to deal with if you weren't," A.J. said in a firm tone. "I also think you've carried this baggage long enough. It's time you moved on."

"I've tried," July whispered, feeling more like a failure than ever.

"I know you have. This is heavy though and I'm thinking you might need some help."

July swiped her sweaty palms against her nightgown. "I want to get past it."

"Then take the first step. Find a counselor you can trust and share your burden with them. Do it because you're strong and because you don't want this to affect your relationship with Adam."

"I don't k—"

"Promise me, July," A.J.'s tone took on an unexpected urgency. "Promise me you'll at least give it a try."

She knew what her friend was saying made sense. But to share her deepest, darkest secrets with a stranger? Then Adam stirred and when her gaze settled on the baby, her baby, she knew she had no choice.

"Promise me, July," he said even more insistently this time.

July took a deep breath and let it out slowly. "I'll do it."

"Good."

"What about David? What should I do about him?"

"For now--nothing. Cut yourself some slack and trust that when the time is right, you'll do what needs to be done."

Her shoulders dropped and she felt some of the tension leave her body. "I love you, A.J."

"What are friends for?" he said in that cavalier tone he used to hide his true feelings from the world.

He didn't tell her he loved her back. She hadn't expected the words. He was that favorite older brother that found it difficult to express his feelings even though you knew he cared. And July knew he cared. That was enough for her.

CHAPTER SIX

David turned onto the highway leading into Jackson, grateful the rain had finally stopped. While he didn't mind helping out Mary Karen by picking up the twins from a birthday party in Wilson, he couldn't wait to drop them off and head home.

It had been a long, tiring week made more stressful by the fact that he'd temporarily lost track of July and Adam. When he'd stopped by the motel where July had been living, he discovered she'd moved out. Still, he was completely confident—well, fairly confident--they were in the area. After all, Adam had an appointment with the pediatrician next week and he'd heard rumors July was starting a new job. But he was annoyed she hadn't given him her new address because now he was going to have to track her down.

"I'm cold, Uncle David," Conner called from the back seat of the Suburban.

"More heat coming right up." David pushed a button and the fan kicked on. Spring came late to this part of the country. While the jackets the boys wore had probably been adequate earlier in the day, they didn't provide near enough warmth for the now thirty-degree temperature.

"We have a new baby at our house," Caleb told him.

"He's really tiny," Conner added.

"That's nice." David smiled. It was just as he'd thought; their "fat" hamster had been more than just overweight. "Tell me about the party."

He kept the boys talking all the way into town. By the time he wheeled the SUV into Mary Karen's driveway, he knew every gift that had been opened. He'd also heard all about the birthday boy eating five pieces of cake before throwing up on his mother's shoes.

Caleb smiled. "It was gross."

"Yeah, gross," Conner agreed.

David chuckled and pulled to a stop behind a Jeep 4x4. The sticker on the bumper told him the vehicle was a rental. Funny, he didn't recall Mary Karen mentioning she was having company this evening.

"Let me out, Uncle David," Conner called.

"I want out, too," Caleb echoed.

Once unbuckled, the boys raced up the walk. His sister opened the door just as the dynamic duo reached the front step.

"Got 'em here safe and sound." David took the door from her hands and held it open while the two rushed inside.

"I'm so glad you're here."

For the first time David noticed the worry furrowing Mary Karen's brow. "What's the matter?"

"I want you to check Logan. He's been clingy all evening. I thought he simply missed his brothers...until I saw his flushed cheeks and felt his forehead."

"What's his temp?"

"One hundred three."

"Let me get my bag." Because of the rural nature of this part of the state, David kept a doctor's bag in the car. He was back on the porch in seconds, shooting his sister a reassuring smile. "Probably just the start of an ear infection, although we have seen some strep." David stepped into the house. "Until we determine what's wrong, you best keep the twins away from him."

"What about Adam?" The feminine voice came from the living room. "Is it safe for him to be in the house?"

He was still processing the voice when July slipped into the living room and met his gaze. For a second David thought he was hallucinating. He'd been thinking of her so much these past few days, it made sense that if he would conjure anyone up, it would be her.

But this woman standing in his sister's living room was no apparition. Dressed casually in a bulky Northwestern sweatshirt and jeans, she looked more like a college coed than a woman who'd had a baby three days ago.

A familiar electricity filled the air. He tried not to stare but couldn't help it. "What are you doing here?"

"She lives with us, Uncle David." Caleb's arms were now wrapped around Henry, the cockapoo.

"Her an' baby Adam," Conner echoed, smacking a noisy kiss on the dog's nose.

He met July's gaze and lifted a brow.

"The boys are right. This is my new home." July glanced around and shrugged. "For now."

David turned to his sister who'd been watching the interchange with unabashed curiosity.

"July and Adam are renting a room from me for the next month or so," Mary Karen said, a fondness for her new tenants evident in her tone. "When she discovered I was your sister I actually thought she was going to change her mind about moving in. David, what in the world did you do to her?"

The words were delivered in a half-joking manner, but there was puzzlement in Mary Karen's eyes.

"I delivered her baby." It wasn't much of a response but David didn't have the inclination to tell his sister the whole story.

"Mary Karen, I told you he didn't do anything," July protested.

"Finding out my doctor was your brother was simply unexpected news."

From the look on her face, unwelcome, too.

Before anyone could say another word a plaintive call rang out.

"Mommy. Mommy."

"The native is getting restless," Granny Fern called out from the back bedroom.

David fixed a gaze on July. "You and Adam stay here. We don't want the baby exposed."

He turned on his heel and without another word strode down the hall, Mary Karen scurrying to catch up.

July watched the two disappear into the bedroom where Granny was tending to Logan. She hoped the child was okay. It wasn't until she'd returned from a short shopping trip that she learned the two-year-old wasn't feeling well. She'd immediately taken Adam to the bedroom they shared.

David was right. If Logan was contagious, Adam shouldn't be around the boy. But where could they go? Most of the motel rooms in the area were booked with skiers.

"False alarm."

July jerked herself back from her worry and found herself face-to-face with David. Her heart skipped a beat. "He's okay?"

"Throat is fine. His ears are red and there's definitely fluid there. Give him twenty-four hours on Amoxil and he'll be back fighting with his brothers."

"Thank you so much for staying, David." Mary Karen rushed past them, coat on, purse and keys in hand. "I promise, I'll be right back."

"There's no reason you have to do this," David protested. "I can go to the drug store and pick up the antibiotic."

From the hint of exasperation in his tone, July got the feeling this wasn't the first time he'd made the offer.

"I'll do it. He's my son. I'll get his prescription." Mary Karen stopped at the door and turned back. "You both help yourself to any of the leftovers."

"You're staying?" July turned to David, unable to keep the surprise from her voice. His coat was still on and she realized she'd hoped he'd follow Mary Karen out the door.

"Yep." He shrugged off his jacket and draped it on the coat tree.

"You've been busy all day," July reminded him. "Don't you want to go home and relax?"

His blue eyes met hers. "Even if I wanted to leave, Mary Karen took my Suburban."

Her heart sank. "Oh."

"How about keeping me company while I see what there is to eat?" The look in his eyes practically dared her to say no.

"Okay." July never could resist a challenge. She glanced in the direction of her bedroom. "After I check on Adam."

"I'll come with you." He put a hand on her elbow. Before July quite knew what was happening, she was propelled down the hall with David too close for comfort. The intoxicating scent of his cologne teased her nostrils and sent her heart rate soaring.

"How do you know which room is mine?" Her voice sounded oddly breathless, even to her ears.

"Easy." He stopped in front of her door. "When I saw the twins' stuff in Logan's room I figured you'd inherited theirs."

"I felt bad when I learned I'd taken over their domain, but Mary Karen assured me they'll be fine." July pushed the door open and paused. Adam slept in the port-a-crib Mary Karen had brought up from the basement. Putting a finger to her lips, she silently crossed the room. Though his blanket sleeper probably kept him warm enough she covered him with a light blanket.

"He's a beautiful baby." David spoke in a low tone.

She cast a sideways glance before returning her attention to her son. Love and pride mixed with a healthy dose of awe filled her. "I can't believe he came out of my body."

"If anyone ever doubts it, I'm your witness." David grinned.

He'd been there with her when Adam was conceived and when he'd taken his first breath. But, she realized as a wave of guilt shot though her, they wouldn't be together when Adam walked. Or said his first words. Or went to kindergarten...

"Uncle David," Caleb called in a loud whisper.

Adam's forehead furrowed but his eyes remained closed. David turned and held up a hand to the little boy.

After one last quick glance to make sure all was well, July grabbed the baby monitor and followed David from the room, gently closing the door behind her.

"Thanks for being so quiet, Caleb." David scrunched down until he was at eye level with the boy. "Did you need something?"

"Me and Connor wondered—"

"Connor and I," David gently corrected.

"Uh, Connor and I wondered if we could watch The Incredibles."

"That should be okay," David said, "but you won't be able to finish it. As soon as your mom gets back, you're coming home with me."

Caleb's blue eyes—so like his uncle's—widened. "We get to have a sleepover?"

"That's the plan." David tousled the boy's blonde hair. "Is that okay with you?"

"Yippee." Caleb bolted down the hall and July could hear him calling for his brother.

July tilted her head. "Don't you have to be at the hospital tomorrow?"

"I have the weekend off." David started down the hall and she fell into place beside him. He shook his head, a little smile on his lips. "I can't remember the last time that happened."

July couldn't hide her shock. "You're going to spend your time off babysitting?"

"Mary Karen will have her hands full with Logan." David shrugged. "And Granny needs her rest."

"But—"

"The boys are no trouble." David paused at the door to the living room where the two were already positioned in front of the television. "They've got their own bedroom at my house and extra clothes, so it's easy."

"You really like kids, don't you?" The realization twisted July's stomach in one big knot.

David chuckled. "You make it sound like a bad thing."

"No. No. It's not." July struggled to explain. "I think it's wonderful."

"They're my nephews," David reminded her. "Family is important to me."

Instead of admiration, July was seized with a cold chill. If she'd had any doubts what having a son might mean to him, she had none now.

Tell him, a tiny voice inside her head urged. Do it.

There was no reason something so simple, so basic, should be so hard. Yet her palms turned sweaty and her heart began to pound.

"Have you eaten?" he asked, giving her an out.

She took it and said a little prayer of thanks for the reprieve. "I had a sandwich and an apple for lunch." July pulled her brows together, replaying the day's events. "Nothing since."

The growl from her stomach told her she'd remembered correctly.

"Follow me to the kitchen."

When they got to the kitchen he gestured to the table. "Have a seat. How does a grilled ham and cheese sound?"

July wasn't sure she'd heard correctly. "You're going to make me a sandwich?"

"It's not a big deal." He shrugged. "I'm going to make one for myself."

While he pulled out the ham and the cheese from the refrigerator, July took a seat. She couldn't remember the last time anyone cooked for her. Certainly her mother had never felt the need to put anything on the table. "Your wife must have been thrilled to have a husband so handy in the kitchen."

"Celeste traveled a lot." David placed an iron skillet on the stove and turned on the heat. "For me, learning to cook became a survival thing."

Celeste. The name sounded like the wife of a doctor.

"Why did she travel so much?"

Was it only her imagination or did the light suddenly leave his eyes?

"She worked as a marketing rep for a company based in LA. Travel was part of her job duties. She loved it. She—" He stopped himself. "Enough about that. We have a more important topic to discuss."

July's breath caught in her throat. Even though David already had the sandwiches in the pan, she stood. Not to run exactly, but surely there was someplace else she needed to be.

"I want to hear how you and Mary Karen got together." He turned the sandwiches. "I didn't know she was looking to rent a room."

July dropped back into her seat and swallowed a nervous giggle. That's what he wanted to discuss? The tension in her shoulders eased and she relaxed against the back of the chair. "The social worker at the hospital gave me Mary Karen's name and phone number."

"Lexi?"

"That's the one." When July had first learned that her new landlord and babysitter was David's sister, she'd felt as if she'd been sold out by the social worker...for all of five minutes. She'd quickly realized how comfortable she was with Mary Karen. "I met with your sister and we immediately hit it off. It was a win-win situation for both of us. She needed the money. I needed a place to live and a babysitter."

David flipped the sandwiches onto the plates he'd placed by the stove. "Milk?"

"Please." Growing up beer and Mountain Dew had been the only "beverages" in the fridge. Milk hadn't even been an option. Until July discovered she was pregnant, she'd rarely drunk anything but coffee and soda. Over the past eight months she'd acquired a taste for the white stuff.

In a matter of minutes, a tall glass of milk and a sandwich were placed before her.

With his own plate in hand, David pulled out a chair and sat opposite her. "Is that why you decided to stay? Your desire to have my sister watch Adam was stronger than the desire to keep your distance from me?"

The words were casual, the tone off-hand and his expression certainly didn't give anything away. But July sensed she'd hurt him with her earlier attitude and the realization only added to her guilt. She told herself it didn't matter, but in the warmth of this kitchen, under the fluorescent light glow, she couldn't help remembering how nice he'd been to her that long ago night, how considerate he'd been in the hospital.

"I like you, David, you know that," July admitted. "I have from the moment we met."

She didn't even need to close her eyes to remember how confident and self-assured—and yes, handsome—he'd looked that night. And the sizzle. Ah, who could forget the electricity…

"Do I hear a call for a truce somewhere in those words?" he teased, though his eyes were watchful.

July chewed her bite of sandwich and swallowed. "Truce."

His blinding smile sent a warm rush of pleasure all the way to the tips of her toes.

"Now that we've got that settled—"

"Got what settled?"

July turned in her seat to find Granny Fern, David's maternal grandmother, standing in the doorway. Not much taller than July, the woman had snow white hair, silver-rimmed eyeglasses and gorgeous skin. She seemed nice enough but was a tad too inquisitive and her assessing gaze made July uncomfortable. She'd never been around seniors and wasn't sure what to expect from this octogenarian who was fiercely protective of her family.

Thankfully, for now, Granny's attention was focused on her grandson. "Where's your sister?"

"She's picking up a prescription for Logan." David rose and pulled out a chair the older woman. "How's he doing?"

"Sleeping...finally." The older woman turned to July. Her hair might be white but those pale blue eyes missed little. "It sounds like you and David have settled your differences."

July cast a sideways glance at David. "No differences."

"That's right. No differences," David added.

"If you say so." Granny's tone was clearly skeptical.

"Would you like something to eat?" David asked, in an obvious attempt to change the subject. "Or drink?"

"I'm fine. You two continue your conversation," Granny said. "You were talking about getting something settled?"

Adam's cry was sweet music to July's ears. She jumped up. "The baby's awake."

"Bring the child in here," Granny urged. "He and I haven't had a chance to get properly acquainted."

July smiled, pleased by the woman's interest. "I'll be back in a second."

But the second turned into minutes. Adam was wet. Though July was becoming more adept at diaper changes, she certainly wasn't an expert. She forgot how little boys sprayed. Only after she'd gotten Adam cleaned up and had changed her own shirt, did she return to the kitchen

David was placing a steaming cup of hot tea in front of his

grandmother when July walked into the kitchen. He looked up when he heard her footsteps and smiled.

Granny held out her frail arms. "May I hold him?"

July hesitated. She'd planned to show her the baby, not hand him over. Still, she didn't want to be an overprotective mother. If Granny was strong enough to tend to a two-year-old power-house like Logan, she could certainly handle a five-pound baby.

The baby had been in the older woman's arms for less than a minute when Granny slipped off his cap. Then, with an intensity that filled July with unease, she spent almost a full minute studying his face. "It's uncanny," she said finally.

David took a bite of sandwich followed by a sip of milk.

Okay, maybe she should have left well enough alone but July was curious. "What's uncanny?"

"Your baby looks exactly like David." Granny tilted her head and met July's gaze with an assessing look. "Is there any chance Adam could be his son?"

CHAPTER SEVEN

Ice replaced the blood in July's veins.

David chuckled. "You think he's mine just because he has dark hair?"

July exhaled the breath she'd been holding. Said that way, it did sound ridiculous.

"Dark hair with a hint of wave," Granny said, refusing to back down. "And a widower's peak."

The bite of sandwich which had been sliding quite nicely down July's throat stopped. To her horror, she began to cough.

David began to rise from his seat but July waved him down. She grabbed the glass of milk and chugged it. So much for keeping her cool. When she could breathe normally again, July managed to reply. "Where were we? Oh yes, widow's peak…or widower's peak…since he's a boy. I've worked with many people who had them. Seems to be fairly common."

"Did you now?" Granny took a sip of tea, not appearing impressed. "You don't have a widow's peak. Anyone in your family have one?"

July shifted in her seat. "Not that I know."

"Then the baby must have gotten it from the father." Granny cast a pointed glance in David's direction.

July refused to look at him. "I never noticed."

"He must have." Granny gently stroked the baby's cheek with a crooked finger. "It's an inherited characteristic."

"My grandmother has a strong interest in anything to do with genealogy," David said.

"I believe a child's heritage gives them a strong foundation in life."

July thought of her mother. Of the father she'd never known. Addict mother. Absent dad.

"I'm sure it plays a part." July rose and took the baby from Granny's arms. Regardless of what happened between her and David, she'd give Adam that strong foundation. His legacy would begin with her. "If you'll excuse me, I'm going to my room. It's time for Adam's feeding."

"Feed him here," Granny urged. "Breastfeeding is natural. There's no need to hide yourself away in a bedroom."

It might be natural but July had no interest in baring her breast with David in the room.

"I'm still getting the hang of it," July told her. "An audience would make me nervous."

David experienced a pang of regret when she left the room. They'd been having a good conversation...until Granny showed up. He pushed the uncharitable thought aside.

"He's a cute little boy," Granny said. "Kind of scrawny but cute."

"Yes, he is."

"It's still odd."

David lifted a brow. "What is?"

"He really is the spitting image of you when you were a baby."

∾

The words played over and over in David's mind all week. While he didn't put much stock in his grandmother's observation, he kept wondering if there was something he'd missed. But he hadn't seen July recently and hadn't gotten a good look at the baby since that night.

Though David knew it was probably pointless, his next day off he headed to Mary Karen's hoping for a few quiet moments to study Adam's face. When he got there, quiet was nowhere to be found.

The place was in an uproar. The baby was crying. The dog was barking. The boys were running through the house shrieking.

David grabbed two of them as they ran by. "No running in the house."

Caleb skidded to a stop beside his brothers. "We're playing 'monster-catch-me.'"

"I don't care what you're playing," David spoke firmly. "Walk. Not run. Understand?"

"Yes." Caleb heaved a frustrated breath.

Connor nodded.

"I sorry," Logan said, though mischief danced in his eyes. The medicine clearly had done its work. The two-year-old appeared back to his high energy self.

David didn't know how Mary Karen handled these boys alone. He firmly believed children needed a dad as well as a mom. Of course, his ex-brother-in-law hadn't gotten that message. He was too busy enjoying the single life back in Boston.

He smiled at his nephews. "Why don't you get out the Lincoln logs and see what you can build me?"

Caleb and Connor exchanges looks then nodded and ran toward the living room with Logan close behind.

"Walk," David called out.

The boys immediately slowed their steps.

"Thank you."

He turned to find Mary Karen in the hallway, Adam wailing loudly in her arms. Her face was as white as the blanket wrapped about the baby. David narrowed his gaze. "You don't look so good."

His sister's lips lifted in a wan smile. "Migraine."

"Let me have him." David took the crying baby, not surprised she didn't protest. "All that screaming can't be helping your headache. Where's Granny?"

"Downtown having coffee with some friends."

"July?"

"Scouting locations," Mary Karen said. "She left early this morning."

"Did you take your medicine?"

"The drugs make me tired and lightheaded." Mary Karen had to raise her voice to be heard above the baby's screams. "I couldn't take the chance of falling with the baby."

"Take the pills and lie down," David ordered in a soothing voice. "I'll watch the boys."

Relief filled her pain-filled eyes. "Are you sure?"

"Get to bed, little sister. In a few hours things will look totally different."

"I owe you."

"I'll add it to your tab."

The response brought a smile to her lips. With a hand to her head, she turned toward her bedroom, leaving David with the screaming infant.

"Granny thinks you look like me." He studied the scrunched up red face and trembling chin. "I have to tell you that I'm not seeing the resemblance. You don't really look like your mom, either."

The baby screamed louder.

He jiggled the infant gently. After a minute, the crying subsided. David continued to talk in a low soothing tone about his week while he searched for a bottle. He found one in the refrigerator behind a carton of juice. He'd assumed that even though July was nursing she had a back-up plan.

David heated the bottle, using the microwave technique his sister had taught him when Logan was a baby. Logan had been a fussy baby and those had been difficult days. David's brother-in-law had packed up and left town. Shortly after that happened, Celeste had died. Working extra shifts and helping Mary Karen with the twins and new baby had kept David busy during the long, lonely months that followed.

After checking the temperature of the milk on the inside of his wrist, David carried the baby into the living room and sank into the overstuffed rocker. From this position he could watch the boys and feed Adam at the same time.

The baby took easily to the bottle, his little face relaxing as he sucked. He smelled clean, like baby powder and fine, dark hair covered his head. Gazing down at the child, David still didn't see a resemblance, but holding him felt right. He wondered now why he and Celeste had chosen to wait, how their travel and their lifestyle could have ever been more important to them than this.

Immune to the tension gripping David's chest, the baby waved his fists in the air and gurgled happily. David blew out a breath and trailed a finger down the infant's soft cheek. One thing was certain, if Adam was his son, he'd never let him go.

～

July returned home a little after five. Though she and her guide had found some great locations, it had been difficult to concentrate. She missed Adam horribly. She hoped that leaving him would eventually get easier. Her only salvation was she trusted Mary Karen to take good care of her son.

Turning the key in the lock, July pushed the door open. The sound of childish laughter brought a smile to her lips. She supposed she could have called out her arrival but instead she simply followed the happy voices to the kitchen.

For several seconds she stood in the doorway absorbing the scene. Granny stood at the counter tossing a salad and chatting with Mary Karen who was busy loading the dishwasher. Adam was in David's arms, contentedly watching the boys as David patiently instructed them in the art of making English muffin pizzas.

The heartwarming family scene could have been lifted straight from a Hallmark movie. A sharp pain lanced July's heart. Sometimes it felt as if she'd spent her entire life on the outside looking in. She sighed and forced a smile to her lips. "Well, well. Look what the cat dragged in. Don't you have your own home?"

David's head jerked at the sound of her voice. He turned and met her gaze, his lips widening into a welcoming smile. He chuckled. "Sometimes I wonder why I bother with one."

"I had a migraine today." Mary Karen glanced at her brother. "David sent me to bed and watched the boys. He was a life saver."

"How's Adam been?"

"Calm now." David smiled. "Just a second ago he was fussing."

"He's probably hungry." It was the wrong thing to say. Just when she thought the moment couldn't get any worse, the mere thought of Adam nursing made her milk flow. July crossed her arms across her chest.

Mary Karen, who'd breastfed all three boys, shot her a knowing smile.

"How was work?" David crossed the room and handed over the baby.

"Found a few locations that are definitely worth revisiting." July smiled down at Adam.

"I hope you didn't overdo," Granny dumped the salad into a large red bowl. "You just had a baby. You make sure they know that."

"I didn't do anything, really," July told her, "except let the guide drive me around. Still, I'm exhausted."

"Most women take six weeks to rest up," Mary Karen reminded her.

"Well, this one doesn't have that luxury." July felt a surge of satisfaction when Adam snuggled contently against her.

David slid a cookie sheet full of mini-pizzas into the oven then straightened. "At least you can come home and relax in the evenings."

"Usually," July admitted. "Not tomorrow, though."

"What's going on tomorrow?" David asked.

"I'm taking candid photos at a Chamber of Commerce event right after I get back from Yellowstone." July hadn't sought out the assignment. The last thing she wanted was to come home, change her clothes and leave again. But Tom, the Chamber hospitality chair, had contacted her. Once again, the money was too good to pass up.

David cocked his head. "Is that the Jackson After-Hours event they hold monthly?"

July shrugged. "All I know is that I'm supposed to show up at a downtown brewery by five with my camera ready."

"It's good to see you getting involved in the community," he said after a long moment.

July let the comment go. Because once her job in Jackson Hole was done, there was nothing keeping her here.

CHAPTER EIGHT

David hadn't been to a Jackson Chamber event in several years. He'd tried to get Celeste interested in the group. That hadn't gone well. Then again, her business wasn't based in Jackson so he'd had to agree there was little point in networking here.

He always hoped that in time she would start meeting people, making friends, putting down roots. Her travel schedule made that difficult. Then she was gone.

David paused at the bottom of the steps leading to the front door of the popular brewery. Laughter and talk floated in the air. How long had it been since he'd just relaxed and socialized with anyone other than family? David thought for a moment. It had been in Chicago, when he'd spent time with July.

Though he could deny it, deep down he knew she was the reason he was here tonight. He wanted to speak to her without Granny and Mary Karen listening to his every word.

Thankfully, for a Friday it had been a slow day in the ER and he'd been able to leave the hospital on time. David climbed the stairs with purposeful steps. Once inside the restaurant he followed the sounds of conversation to the bar. There were a few grey-haired businessmen and women in attendance but most were young professionals in their thirties and forties.

Though the area was packed, he spotted July immediately. Dressed in a green silky shirt, black pants and high-heeled boots, she fit in perfectly, yet still stood out. Maybe it was the red cast to her hair. Or perhaps the proud, confident stance. Whatever it was, just like in Chicago, he found himself intensely aware of her.

After grabbing a glass of beer, David made his way through the crowd. Though he stopped several times along the way to talk, he kept July firmly in his sight. She'd occasionally snap a few pictures but seemed more interested in the man at her side than in working.

David recognized the guy flirting with her. Tom Harding was the manager of one of the sporting goods stores in town. With messy sun-bleached blonde hair and sporting a year-round tan, Tom always looked more like a ski bum than a responsible husband and father. Although he had a perfectly lovely wife, rumor was Tom still liked the ladies. From the attention he was lavishing on July, it appeared the rumor had some validity.

A surge of something that felt an awful lot like jealously rose up inside David. He told himself it was merely a protective urge. She was a guest in his sister's home and new to town. And then, there was still the possibility they shared a baby together.

David made his way to the end of the shiny mahogany bar where July now stood with her back to him. As he drew close a look of surprise crossed Tom's face. "I sure didn't expect to see you here tonight. Still doing the triathlons?"

While the man's tone was friendly enough, the proprietary way he glanced at July told David he didn't appreciate being interrupted.

"Last triathlon I did was Pinedale," David informed him. "I'm planning on competing in a couple marathons this summer."

July whirled at the sound of his voice. The surprise in her eyes told him Tom wasn't the only one who hadn't expected to see him.

"July, here," Tom gestured with his head toward the red-head, "has been a casual runner and she's interested in getting in marathon shape. I offered to do some one-on-one training sessions with her."

The lecherous hint in the man's eye told David exactly what he had in mind for those sessions. The fact that he was even talking about running told David that July had failed to mention she'd just had a baby. It would be a good month before she would be released by her doctor to do more than walk.

"Hello, July," David said when Tom made no attempt to do introductions.

If July felt the energy sizzling in the air between them, it didn't show. "Hello, David."

Tom's brows slammed together. "You know each other?"

"She lives at my sister's house." David kept his tone as offhand as hers.

"Tom has done quite a few marathons." July took a sip of club soda and gazed at him over the top of her glass. "Isn't that nice of him to offer to help me?"

David tightened his fingers around his drink. If he didn't know better, he'd think she was trying to make him jealous. He kept his expression neutral and focused on Tom. "I'm surprised you have time for that."

"I've got a good crew at the store." Tom slanted a smile at July. "Most nights I'm out of there by five."

"Doesn't Teresa expect you home?"

July lifted a brow. "Teresa?"

"His wife," David said. "They have a beautiful baby girl. What's her name…Sarah?"

"Samantha," Tom said stiffly. "I was just about to pull out the pictures when you walked up."

From the skeptical look in July's eyes, she didn't believe the lie any more than David did.

"It's been great visiting with you, July." Tom's gaze slid around the crowded room. "But it's time for me to mingle. Stop in the store sometime."

July offered up a non-committal smile and lifted a hand in farewell.

"I didn't mean to chase him away."

July waved a dismissive hand and David experienced a surge of satisfaction.

"I thought you came to take pictures," David said in a conversational tone. "From the little I've observed that camera on the bar isn't getting much action."

July sat down her glass and gazed over the throng of people. "I took quite a few at the beginning but then everyone started to pose. I thought I'd give it a rest for a while. Tom approached me and we got to talking about marathons."

"You could have asked me if you had questions about running." He inhaled the clean, fresh scent of her and his body stirred. "Did I mention I'm looking for a new running, ah walking, partner?"

If she was surprised by the change in subject, it didn't show. A thoughtful look crossed. "When do you go out?"

"Early morning. Before I head to the hospital." He took a sip of beer. An early morning run had been his habit for as long as he could remember. Celeste had run with him several times when they were dating, but had lost interest when her work schedule became more demanding.

"I need to get back into shape…" July admitted.

He jerked his attention back to her. Placing his glass on the bar, David spoke without thinking. "You look pretty good to me."

A becoming shade of pink cut a swath across her cheeks. "You know what I mean…back in running shape. If I have to walk for a while to build up, that's okay, too."

"There's nothing like knowing someone is waiting for you to help get you out of bed in the morning," he said in his most persuasive tone.

To his surprise she appeared to be considering his proposition when her phone rang. It was an odd ring—a theme from some musical—but one she seemed to instantly recognize.

She pulled the phone from her bag, her lips lifting in a smile. "I'm sorry," she said, not looking sorry at all. "It's my friend A.J. We've been playing telephone tag today."

A band of steel wrapped around David's chest and began to tighten. He hadn't known the two were in contact.

Returning her attention to the phone, July answered in a cheery tone, "Hey, you. We finally connect."

With a tiny wave she stepped out of earshot, cradling the phone lovingly in her hand. David knew he should look away, but it was like watching a train wreck. Even when she turned her back to him, he couldn't pull his gaze from her. Her laughter floated above the conversational din and the tightness in his chest made breathing nearly impossible.

They'd been making progress. For a second he actually thought she was going to agree to meet him in the morning. Spending time with her would have been a good thing, a way to get to know her better. Because if it turned out they did share a baby, there would be all sorts of details to work out, like custody and visitation.

The strong desire to be with her didn't have a thing to do with how much he enjoyed her company or how alive he felt in her presence. Not one thing.

～

The sky was awash in shades of orange and yellow as the sun began to rise over the flat range lands of the National Elk Refuge just outside of Jackson. July could see her breath in the barely-above-freezing temperatures but in Mary Karen's running jacket and microfiber pants, she wasn't the least bit cold.

David, keeping pace beside her, showed no signs of chill, but that didn't surprise her. When their paths had crossed, he'd already run five miles and insisted he was ready to walk.

He hadn't looked winded, much less cold. He'd told her he normally ran this route but this was her fourth day out and yet the first time she'd seen him. When he'd asked if he could join her, it seemed rude to say no. And this could be her opportunity to tell him the truth…if she could only get up the nerve.

She glanced sideways at him, at the classically handsome profile, and experienced an unexpected surge of yearning. For what she wasn't sure.

They'd talked for the first mile. But for the past twenty minutes they'd walked in companionable silence. Still, she sensed something weighed on his mind.

"You might as well tell me," July said as they rounded a bend in the deserted road that wound its way through the refuge.

"What are you talking about?" His breath came easily which confirmed this killer walking pace wasn't nearly as taxing on him as it was on her.

"You want to ask me something." It wasn't a question, but a statement of fact.

Without warning he laughed. "Am I that easy to read?"

She smiled. "Just spit it out."

"In a little over two weeks my great-grandmother will be recognized for sixty years of Sunday School service."

"Old news," July said, relieved it didn't have anything to do with Adam. "Mary Karen already took her shopping for a new dress."

July had been surprised at all the preparation the two were doing. It appeared this award was a big deal.

"I was thinking it'd be nice if you and Adam came." His words picked up speed as if he was afraid she'd say no without proper thought. "The whole family will be there."

The whole family. Meaning all the ones she knew as well as David's parents. Mary Karen's boys could talk of little else other than their grandparents' return from their European cruise. Or, as the boys called it, their "big boat ride."

While July was sure "Bob" and "Linda" were nice people, she felt awkward becoming any more involved with this family than she already was…

"I appreciate the invitation," she began. "But—"

"But--" he prompted when she didn't continue.

"Adam and I are already too close to all of you as it is." The last few words came out on a sigh.

"I don't understand…"

"The boys treat Adam like a baby brother. Do you know he already recognizes them?"

"Of course he does. He sees them all the time. But that's about Adam," David said. "What about you?"

July paused and thought for a moment. "Well, Granny bosses me around like I'm one of her grandkids. Mary Karen treats me like a sister."

Though her tone held a hint of exasperation, the truth was she rather liked feeling like part of the family. It was a novel experience and for her a pleasurable one.

"I bet I know what you're going to say next," David said with a wry smile, "that being with me is like hanging out with a favorite brother."

The thought was so ridiculous, July laughed out loud. "Believe me, the feelings you bring out in me are anything but brotherly."

David stopped so suddenly that July was several steps past him before she realized it. She turned. "What's wrong?"

"Then I'm not the only one feeling the pull."

July smiled. "I blame mine on post-partum hormone surges. I'm not sure what fuels yours."

"I like you, July." David took a step closer. "Isn't that enough of a reason?"

Though her feet itched to sprint down the road, she stood absolutely still. Her heart fluttered. "You don't know me."

"You're wrong," he said. "You and I spent some good quality time together in Chicago…and not just in bed." He took another step toward her. "I definitely know you well enough to know I like you."

She swallowed; her mouth suddenly dry as dirt. Growing close to this man was dangerous, with a capital D. Still, desire surged and she couldn't make herself move away.

"The question is, is it well enough to kiss you again?" He now stood so near there was no distance between them. He curled his fingers and tilted back her chin, gazing into her eyes.

Ever so slowly—giving her plenty of time to step back or say no—he lowered his lips to hers.

The kiss started out slow, as if they had all the time in the world. He caressed her skin with his mouth, planting gentle kisses on her lips, her jaw and down her neck while his hands remained respectfully on her shoulders.

He nibbled her ear lobe then moved back to her tingling lips. She opened her mouth and when he still didn't deepen the kiss, she slid her tongue into his mouth. That's when the world exploded.

By the time he stepped back, July was trembling. She raised a shaky hand to her head. "Wow" was the only word she could get out.

David stared, his blue eyes dark and unreadable. "Wow, indeed."

Though she wanted to kiss him again, the heat flowing through her veins told her she wouldn't be satisfied with just another kiss. The realization sent red flags popping up. The safe thing, the sensible response was to head home. Besides, her secret was making her feel awkward and she still had to feed Adam before she left for Yellowstone.

Without a word, July turned and began walking toward town. In several long strides, David was at her side.

"What do you think?" he asked.

"About the kiss?"

He nodded.

She lifted a shoulder in a slight shrug. "It was okay."

"For me, too," he said with a grin.

He didn't speak again until they reached the gate leading out of the refuge. "What about church? Will you come?"

July didn't need to even think about this one. Though she sensed this was important to him, she couldn't go to church. Not with him. Not with his family. Not until she'd told him the truth. "I—we—don't belong--"

"If you think I want Adam there because I think he could be my son, that's not it at all." His tone was matter-of-fact and almost believable. "I'm asking because it would mean a lot to Granny to have you there."

"I'm sorry, David, but the answer is—"

"Don't decide now." He reached around her and opened the gate. "Two weeks is a long time. Just think about it. That's all I ask."

"You don't give up easily, do you?"

He grinned. "Not when it's something I want."

Strong and determined. July found the qualities appealing. But that personality type usually had high expectations, not only of themselves but of others. Which made July wonder what David would think of her when he discovered that she was flawed and weak?

~

Though the photo of the majestic grizzly she'd snapped in Yellowstone should have been in the forefront of her mind, all July had been able to think about was David and what had happened in the Elk Refuge that morning.

She pulled the rental jeep to a stop in the supermarket lot and hopped out. Lowering her head against the brisk north wind she fought her way to the front of the store, wondering exactly when it was that she'd lost her mind.

Was it when she'd put David's name on the birth certificate as Adam's father? Or perhaps when she decided to move in with Mary Karen despite finding out she was David's sister? No, it had to be the kiss. Considering the chemistry between them it was a wonder they'd made it out of the Elk Refuge with their clothes on.

Of course, she reassured herself as she grabbed a shopping basket, she'd stopped it after one kiss...or anyway, before the clothes came off. If she ran into him tomorrow morning she'd simply turn and—

"July. What a pleasant surprise." Lexi stood a few feet in front of her, a sack of groceries in one hand and a small girl in the other.

"Hello, Lexi." July smiled. "I haven't seen you since I was discharged from the hospital."

"Yes, well, about that—" Lexi handed her daughter several quarters and pointed to a nearby gumball machine. She waited until the girl had scampered just out of earshot to say more. "Are you angry with me?"

July saw worry in the social worker's eyes. Though it would have been nice to have all the facts up front, all July felt was gratitude. "Mary Karen is wonderful. The house is nice, the rent reasonable and she's very good with Adam. Thank you so much for the referral."

Lexi twisted her purse straps in her hands. "I should have told you she was David's sister."

"It was a shock." July admitted.

"Mommy. Mommy. I got me a blue one," Lexi's daughter called out. "I hope the next one is red."

Lexi watched her daughter put a third quarter in the machine. The child's dark brows were furrowed and her expression intense. It was as if she was trying to "will" the machine to give her the color she wanted.

"She looks just like you," July said.

"That's what everyone says." Lexi's expression softened. "Addie is a mini-me."

"Granny says Adam looks just like David as a baby."

"She knows?" The look of shock on Lexi's face would have been laughable at any other time.

"Suspects." July glanced down at the shopping basket in her hands. "They'll all know soon enough."

"You're going to tell them?"

"I'm going to tell David…before I leave Jackson."

"I know it's none of my business, but I don't understand why you're waiting."

"I have my reasons."

"Oh my goodness." Lexi's eyes widened and July followed the direction of her gaze just in time to see Addie stick her hand—and most of her arm--up inside the machine. "Addison Marie, stop that this instant."

"I'd better let you go—"

Lexi's hand on her arm stopped her retreat.

"July, I'm sorry I didn't tell you about Mary Karen being David's sister from the beginning. My only excuse is that I really believed it was the perfect place for you and thought you wouldn't give her a chance if you knew she was David's sister."

The words flowed from Lexi's lips like a fast-moving river that had been dammed up and had just been re-opened. "My decision to hold back that information walked the line of ethical behavior. If the situation had been reversed, I'd have wanted to know. Can you forgive me?"

"Yes. Of course I forgive you." The sincerity in the social worker's voice tugged at July's heart strings. "I have no hard feelings."

As she accepted Lexi's apology, July realized this is how it should be. If you wronged someone, you asked for their forgiveness. It shouldn't have to be so difficult...

"Maybe you and I could get together for coffee sometime?" The hopeful gleam in the social worker's eyes took July by surprise.

"I'd like that." July smiled. It had been a long time since she'd had a girlfriend. "I'll give you a call the first of the week and we'll set something up."

"Perfect." Lexi hesitated. "As long as you don't mind if I bring Addie with me. After working all day, I don't like to leave her with a sitter at night."

"No problem at all." July offered the social worker an understanding smile. "I planned on bringing Adam with me for the same reason."

The two exchanged a smile and a warmth filled July. Her intuition told her she and Lexi stood a good chance of becoming friends. It was a new experience. Oh, she had A.J., but being friends with a guy was different. What was crazy was that in the short time she'd been in Jackson she'd put down more roots than she had during the twenty-six years she'd lived in Chicago.

The time here could be the start of a better life for her. A richer, fuller one than she'd known before. If she was strong enough to take that first step...

July reached out and grabbed Lexi's coat sleeve when she turned to go. "One more thing."

"Yes?" Lexi smiled.

"Do you know the name of a good counselor?"

CHAPTER NINE

Last night July had told A.J. about her appointment with the counselor, but they'd been talking for almost a half hour and he hadn't mentioned it yet. Not that she really wanted to talk about it. She glanced at the clock on her bedside stand. "It's getting late. I suppose--"

"How did the therapy session go?" A.J. asked.

It was a good thing she'd arrived early. She'd sat in her car for fifteen minutes before she'd gotten up the nerve to walk inside. "Okay, I guess."

"That bad?" Disappointment filled his voice. "Just because that one didn't work out doesn't mean—"

"No. No. He worked out just fine," July reassured him. "Dr. Allman reminds me of a teddy bear. It was like talking to Winnie the Pooh."

"How much did you tell him?"

"Everything." Her session was supposed to last fifty minutes but she'd been there almost two hours. She'd relayed her story matter-of-factly, without embellishment. "I cried a little. I was embarrassed. He told me tears always tell us something and we can learn from them."

"Really?"

July smiled. A.J. had never been big on tears. Neither had she for that matter.

"Did you feel better afterwards?" he asked. "Are you seeing him again?"

"Yes and yes." July leaned back against the pillows she'd propped against the headboard and kicked off her shoes. "It's not cheap but you're right. We—I've—got to get rid of this baggage."

"Good for you," A.J. said sounding strangely subdued. "What did he suggest you do about David?"

"He gave me homework. Can you believe it?" July laughed aloud but stopped when Adam stirred. "I'm supposed to apologize to an inanimate object then work my way up. Sort of a desensitization kind of therapy."

"I don't get it."

July hadn't understood it either until Dr. Allman had patiently explained it to her; not only how to do it but the theory behind it. "Instead of starting out with David, I apologize to some object; say one of Adam's toys. Then when that goes okay, I move on to the dog, then to my baby. The goal is to work my way up to David. It makes sense to me."

"That's what matters," A.J. said. "You'll have to let me know how it works. I'll be pulling for you."

"Thank you, A.J." July's heart overflowed with emotion; thankful she had such a good friend. "I'm also supposed to start sharing things about my childhood, easy things first. I thought I'd start with you."

"Me? There's nothing I don't know about you."

"Yes, there is." July tightened her fingers around the phone and reminded herself that this was A.J. and he was safe. "You, Adam Soto, are the reason I made it to adulthood. There were many, many times I didn't want to go on that I wanted to hang it up, but you were always there rooting me on. I'm grateful."

"Yeah, well..."

She'd made him uncomfortable and she was feeling a bit awkward too. It was definitely time to change the subject. "How's Selena? Are you two still hot and heavy?"

He took a moment to respond. "You know how it is after you've been together a while..."

"I'm not sure I do."

"Chicks want the words," he said, exhaling a frustrated breath.

"Are you saying she wants to hear you say you love her?"

"I don't get into that stuff. You know that."

The disgust in his voice made her smile. "Do you? Love her, I mean?"

Just when she'd given up hope of him admitting anything he answered. "Yeah, I guess."

"You guess? Or you know?"

A.J. expelled a harsh breath. "I know. Okay?"

"Far be it for me to give advice." July chose her words carefully. "But maybe you could use the same techniques the counselor gave me."

"I ain't tellin' a damned stuffed toy that I love it, if that's what you're suggesting," A.J. blustered. "No way."

"Just consider it." The clock in the living room began to chime. "I'd better go. Morning will be here all too soon. I love you."

"Yeah, well, later."

July smiled. Regardless of his initial resistance, she knew A.J. would consider her suggestion. She hoped he'd not only consider it but give it a try. It was time both of them got rid of their unwanted baggage.

David reached the gate leading out of the Elk Refuge and stopped to stretch. He hadn't seen July in three days. Not since the morning he'd kissed her right where he stood now. Instead of returning to his normal route, he'd continued to come to the Refuge in the morning, hoping their paths would cross. So far, no July.

He wasn't sure if she'd quit running or had changed locations. Maybe after talking with A.J. she'd regretted the kiss and decided to keep her distance.

David tightened his lips. The guy called himself her friend. Yet he hadn't come to Jackson to see her or Adam. At first, he'd wondered if A.J. was Adam's father. Now that seemed doubtful. Wouldn't a dad at least want to see his offspring?

July's little boy deserved better. He was an amazing baby. Alert and intelligent yet easy going. Any man would be proud to call him son.

Of course, David had to admit he might be a little prejudiced. He'd known Adam was special from the moment the baby had struggled to take his first breath. July, well, she was something special, too. He wanted to stop over and see her and Adam but he didn't want to wear out his welcome.

Besides, July's earlier comment had scored a direct hit. He had been spending too much time at Mary Karen's. He had his own home and his own life.

If that life wasn't as robust and full as he'd like, well, that was his fault. In the meantime, he and Travis would be bringing pizza over to Mary Karen's on Friday night.

The knowledge that he'd get to see July and Adam then would sustain him.

Granny was just leaving for a card party with her friends when July got back from Yellowstone on Friday. It had been a frustrating, non-productive day. The last thing she wanted was to participate in a young mother's book club. But when Mary Karen had heard about July's plans to get together with Lexi, she'd come up with another idea. She'd suggested the three of them form their own book club and include Kayla Simpson, a new mom with a child born with a congenital heart defect.

They planned to meet monthly and the first meeting was tonight. July saw no need to mention that by the time the next meeting rolled around she'd be gone.

As she pushed open the door, she wondered what time David would be stopping by. Last night Mary Karen had told her he'd agreed to take his nephews for the evening.

Her heart picked up speed. She hadn't seen David all week. She glanced down at her jeans and long-sleeved shirt. Perhaps if she hurried, she'd have time to freshen up before he arrived.

July made her way through the house and found Mary Karen in the kitchen with a big stack of paper plates in each hand. Her face brightened when she saw July.

"Perfect timing. Which do you prefer?" Mary Karen raised her right hand. "Fuchsia?" She lifted the other. "Or blue-and-yellow striped?"

July didn't have to think. "Fuchsia."

Mary Karen nodded her agreement. "That's my favorite, too."

July's gaze dropped to the infant seat where Adam slept peacefully. "Wow, he's sure zonked out."

"Blame it on the twins. They played with him all afternoon," Mary Karen smiled. "You should have a few minutes before he wakes up. If you help me set the table before everyone gets here, I'll take care of the drinks."

July pulled her brows together and took the plates from Mary Karen's right hand. "I thought Lexi and Kayla weren't coming until seven."

"They aren't." Mary Karen turned and opened the refrigerator, her words muffled as she stuck her head inside. "I invited David and Travis for pizza at five-thirty. I figured if they were watching the boys for me, I should at least feed them."

Mary Karen pulled out a jug of milk. "Actually, we're only

providing the drinks. When I mentioned I'd run across this fabulous recipe for a Cajun tofu and roasted red pepper pizza, Travis insisted the men supply pizza." Her lips curved up in a smile and she chuckled. "The man has no sense of adventure."

July wondered if Mary Karen realized how often she smiled when speaking of Travis. Adam started to fuss but she finished putting down the plates before walking over to the infant seat. She took a deep breath and stared into his tear-filled eyes. "I'm sorry mommy made you wait."

He stared at her for a moment then smiled, his arms waving in the air. July exhaled the breath she'd been holding. That hadn't been too difficult.

Earlier in the week she'd apologized to his rattle when she'd dropped it on the floor. Flushed by that success she'd moved onto Henry, the cockapoo. Yesterday she'd bumped into the dog in the hall. He'd licked her hand when she told him she was sorry.

She picked Adam up and cuddled him against her breast. He immediately began to root. July dropped into the nearest chair and unbuttoned her shirt experiencing a surge of triumph. In seconds Adam was nursing contentedly. What a difference a few weeks made, she thought to herself. When she'd first brought Adam home, she'd always gone in to her room to feed him. But the atmosphere in the house was so comfortable and accepting, it seemed ridiculous to shut herself off from the others.

July gently stroked her son's fine dark hair. "I didn't know Dr. Fisher was into babysitting."

It was a silly statement that she regretted the moment the words left her mouth. She barely knew the young doctor and certainly had no knowledge of his feelings toward children.

Mary Karen dropped ice into some of the glasses. "He's just along for the ride. They're planning on taking the boys to the movie theater downtown. Travis is like a big kid. He's a sucker for those animated movies."

"He's also a good-looking guy." July strove to keep her tone casual. "Don't you agree?"

Mary Karen confiscated a package of plastic silverware from a drawer and began placing the utensils on the table. Her hair swung forward, hiding her expression. "A lot of women think so."

"I didn't ask about other women," July said pointedly. "I asked if you think so."

The young mother turned and leaned back at the counter. "What is it you really want to know?"

July smiled. "I'm trying to figure out if you're interested in him romantically."

Mary Karen's eyes widened. She looked at July as if she'd lost her mind. Then she laughed. "I have three little boys under the age of five. Romance is not an option."

"You're young." July wasn't sure exactly how old Mary Karen was, but they'd graduated from high school the same year.

The smile faded from Mary Karen's lips and the eyes that met July's were suddenly serious. "I don't feel young. I'll turn twenty-six in August and I'm already dreading it."

"Why?"

Mary Karen shrugged.

"C'mon, tell me," July urged.

"Most women aren't even married at this age. I'm already divorced." Mary Karen dropped her eyes to the table as if she was about to admit a deep dark secret. "Despite everything my husband did, a part of me hoped he would come to his senses and realize what he was giving up."

"Do you still love him?" July asked softly.

"A part of me will always love him. He's the father of my boys." A look of sadness swept across Mary Karen's beautiful face. "If you're asking if I want him back, the answer is no. The man I loved and married would never have deserted his family."

July wanted to find out more but the door in the foyer

creaked open and the sound of deep masculine laughter wafted into the kitchen.

Alarmed, July glanced down at Adam, whose eyes were now closed. She gently unlatched him from her breast and had just pulled her shirt shut when David and Travis strolled into the kitchen.

David looked more like he was going out on a date than taking three rambunctious boys to the movies. July felt a rush of arousal. His thick dark hair still held a hint of dampness, as if he'd just stepped from the shower and toweled off. She had no doubt that if she got close, he'd smell as good as he looked.

Her heart flip-flopped when he shifted his attention to her. "Hello, David."

"Hey, slacker," he taunted. "Haven't seen you at the Refuge lately."

Okay, so she was a coward and he was calling her on it, in a very nice way of course. But she knew without a doubt that if she showed up at the Refuge they'd kiss again.

"I decided to check out another route." She kept the response deliberately vague, not convinced running into him that morning had been mere coincidence.

"Good for you," he spoke as if it didn't matter that he hadn't seen her in almost a week. His gaze shifted to his friend who was holding three large pizza boxes. "We tried to get tofu, Mary Karen, but they were all out."

"Har, har." Mary Karen took the boxes from Travis. "Hello, Trav. It's been too long."

"I agree," he said, flashing a smile then launching into the relative merits of bean curd.

That led to David and Travis reminiscing about some long-ago dinner Mary Karen had made for them. One story led to another but somehow, despite the banter, the pizza and salad and drinks got on the table. The boys were strung tight, the twins vying for David and Travis' attention.

"What's up with the boys tonight?" July asked Mary Karen as they stood at the counter adding cool whip to chocolate pudding.

"They get all geared up when guys are around," Mary Karen said with a shrug.

"Travis seems nice." July smiled. "He was more than agreeable when I asked him to hold Adam."

"He is nice. I've known Trav since high school," Mary Karen dropped her voice even lower. "He was the first boy I ever kissed."

"What are you two beautiful ladies whispering about?" Travis called from the table.

"We were talking about how good looking you are," Mary Karen said with a straight face.

"And about kissing," July added. The second the words left her mouth she wished she could call them back. But that was impossible. All that was left was damage control.

Both men turned and suddenly she had their full attention.

David cocked his head. "What about kissing?"

"I love the way babies kiss," July improvised.

Travis lifted a brow.

"You know," July said, "with their mouths open."

Travis laughed. "I like to kiss like that, too." He jammed an elbow into David's side. "How about you?"

David's eyes locked on July and heat shot like wildfire through her body. How could anyone forget that night in the hotel room? The open-mouthed kisses he'd planted along her inner thigh. Higher and higher until...

"July, are you okay?" Mary Karen's concerned voice was like a splash of cold water. "Your cheeks are bright red."

July slanted a quick sideways glance just in time to see the dimple in David's left cheek flash.

"I'm fine." Though July knew she was playing with fire she dipped her finger into the cup of pudding in front of her. With deliberate slowness she placed the finger in her mouth and let her tongue swirl around it. "Just a little hot."

The fire in David's eyes confirmed he recalled every detail of that night too. She'd told herself many times since, that given the chance to do it all again, she'd never have gone up to his room. She realized she'd only been lying to herself.

Because right here, right now, with the incredible energy surging between them, July knew if she had it to do all over again, she wouldn't hesitate. The way Dr. David Wahl made her feel defied logic.

That's exactly why staying away from him was simply not an option.

CHAPTER TEN

At six-thirty the doorbell rang. Mary Karen dropped her piece of pizza and hurried to the front door.

July sat back in her chair. She carefully wiped her lips with a paper napkin, feeling full and very content.

"Don't tell me you're only going to eat one piece," David teased. "We have another whole pizza that hasn't been touched."

"I don't know what to tell you other than pizza for breakfast can be quite tasty." July wondered if it was wrong to feel so relaxed. Though earlier in the week she'd had concerns about spending more time with David, dinner had been fun.

Travis had regaled them with high school pranks he and David had pulled. Mary Karen had chimed in with some memories of her own. July had been content to simply listen.

Voices sounded in the foyer. July had barely turned in her seat when Kayla and her husband John, with baby Emma in his arms, strolled into the room.

"I'm sorry," Kayla said with an apologetic smile. "I told John tonight is a woman's event."

"I'm not staying," John assured them all. "But I saw David and Trav's vehicles out front and thought I'd say hello."

"Stay and have pizza," David urged. "We've got plenty."

John hesitated but Mary Karen was already pushing him toward a chair. "Sit down."

Mary Karen had barely brought out extra plates when Lexi arrived with Addie in tow. She, too, was easily persuaded to enjoy a slice of pizza.

July sipped her cola and marveled at how different this was from the parties her mother used to throw. Those events always had an abundance of alcohol, drugs and kinky sex. When she knew about them ahead of time, she'd crash at a friend's house. For the impromptu parties, she locked and barricaded her bedroom door.

There had never been parties like this...unless she counted the short time she'd spent with the Kozac family while in emergency foster care. The older couple—at the time they must have been in their early fifties--hosted card parties the first Saturday of the month. The atmosphere at those events had been much like this—warm and inviting.

July resisted the urge to sigh. What would it have been like to grow up in such surroundings? To have that security? To be embraced by family and friends?

After downing a third piece of pizza, John glanced at his watch. "Looks like it's time for Emma and me to hit the road."

The patter of rain, which had begun shortly after Lexi's arrival, now beat against the roof.

"We should go, too," David said making no move to get up.

July didn't blame him for being in no hurry. She also knew Mary Karen wouldn't allow a mere cloudburst to impact the first meeting of her book club.

"You guys can stay if you want," Mary Karen finally said. "I thought we'd meet in the kitchen which means you can have the living room and the television. Perhaps Addie, since she's the oldest, could choose the movie."

Addie's pretty hazel eyes lit up. "Could I, Mommy?"

Lexi hesitated. "I know you guys didn't plan on watching my daughter—"

"What's one more?" David smiled. "In fact, we can take Adam, too. That way you ladies can talk uninterrupted."

July was about to politely turn down the offer when she saw Lexi's face. If she refused to let David watch Adam, Lexi wouldn't allow him to watch Addie either.

"Sure." July rose and handed her son over to David. "Uhh, thank you."

David shot her a wink. "Uhh, you're welcome."

"We'll clean up in here." Travis put a hand on Mary Karen's arm. "You get ready for your book club."

July glanced at David, rounding up the children, Adam asleep against his chest.

Yesterday or even earlier today, she'd have found the scene troubling, but tonight, for whatever reason, it felt…right.

David turned back for a second and their eyes locked.

"I'll take good care of him," he mouthed.

July smiled. Of that she had no doubt.

"That went quicker than I thought," Mary Karen said as the last man left the kitchen and the four women took their places at the table.

"This arrangement works out great for me," Kayla admitted. "Because of Emma's cardiac problems, I know John will feel more comfortable with me in the next room."

"How's the tube feedings going?" Lexi asked.

"Good," Kayla said. "It looks like we'll have to keep the tube in until she's big and strong enough for her heart surgery. Right now, she doesn't have the energy to swallow."

They talked for a couple minutes about Emma's medical issues before Lexi spoke up.

"I like this arrangement, too," she said. "I'd brought some stuff along for Addie to play with, but I'm sure she's having more fun watching the movie and playing with the boys."

July took a sip of the iced tea Mary Karen had set out and just smiled.

"I'm not sure how this club is supposed to work," Kayla admitted. "I enjoyed the one you picked, Mary Karen. The chapter that dealt with adoption really hit home for me."

The book had been on July's "to-do" list but the time just hadn't been there. From the back cover blurb and the inside of the dust jacket, the book appeared focused on successful parenting. It seemed odd that adoption would even be mentioned.

"I'm curious." July inclined her head. "Why did you find the topic so relevant? Were you adopted?"

"No." Kayla shook her head. "But John and I struggled with infertility for years. We had our names in at a number of adoption agencies."

Lexi nodded. "Too many mothers keep them for all the wrong reasons."

July shifted uncomfortably in her seat and told herself she was keeping Adam for all the right reasons.

"What you're saying is they don't look at what's best for the child." Mary Karen's gaze grew thoughtful. "They keep the baby because they can't imagine their life without it or because of the welfare money."

"I can so relate," Kayla confessed. She leaned forward and rested her forearms on the table. "My mother was a single parent with no marketable job skills. She struggled to put food on the table and a roof over our heads."

"That had to have been hard." Sympathy crossed Mary Karen's face.

"It was," Kayla agreed. "While I applaud her efforts, I grew up with this cloud of uncertainty over my head. One summer, we lived out of our car."

"That uncertainty is difficult on a child." Normally July didn't share specific details about her childhood, but she remembered Dr. Allman's homework assignment. "I can relate to your story, Kayla. I spent a lot of my childhood in and out of foster care. All I wanted was a home. A real home. Not an apartment we had to leave every time my mom got behind on the rent. There was one family who wanted to adopt me. They could have given me that home."

"Why didn't they?" Mary Karen asked, her face soft with sympathy.

"My mother refused to relinquish me."

"There are ways to terminate parental rights," Lexi said, sounding very much like a social worker.

"I know there are." July thought back to that time. "But the couple didn't want me bad enough to fight the system. I ended up back with my mother."

"I'm sorry that happened to you." Mary Karen covered July's hand with her own. Her gaze then shifted to encompass the other two women at the table. "We've all had our trials. But we're here to support each other, to learn from each other and hopefully to be the best parent we can be."

Even as July nodded and the talk returned to the book, she found herself thinking of Adam and his future. There was no doubt in her mind that life was going to be tough when they returned to Chicago.

If she was still working at the Sun Times with set hours, a regular paycheck and great benefits, she wouldn't have to worry. Instead, she was a freelancer with an unsteady job and no family for backup if she stumbled. What kind of life could she offer the little boy she loved so much? Was she being selfish to want to take him with her when he could have a wonderful life in Jackson with his dad? The kind of life she'd dreamed of as a child?

Adam deserved to have a house with a yard and a play set out back. He deserved to grow up surrounded by aunts and cousins and grandparents. He deserved the kind of life she'd never be able to give him.

But dear God, could she really leave him behind?

~

David couldn't hide his surprise when Mary Karen strolled into the living room at ten past nine and announced the first meeting of the book club had ended.

Though he and Travis had planned to take Mary Karen's boys to the movies, he'd enjoyed this evening in front of the television even more. The boys had been disappointed about the movie, until he'd convinced them they could have their own party in the living room.

He settled his gaze on the petite red-head standing in the doorway saying good-bye to Lexi and Addie. She'd been okay earlier in the evening but something was definitely troubling her now. Her eyes didn't have that familiar mischievous glint. Not to mention she hadn't asked for Adam back.

David glanced down at the little guy in his arms. There was already a connection between them and every hour he spent with the baby only solidified that bond. The buzzing of his phone made the child stir. Though David wasn't on call tonight he retrieved it from his pocket and glanced at the number. Pressing the button to silence the noise, he let it go to voice mail.

"Nothing important?" Travis raised a brow.

"Just Celeste's old boss," David said. "I have nothing to say to him."

"Why is he calling?" Travis downed the last of his soda. "It's been over two years."

"He left a couple messages. Says he wants to talk." David gently stroked the baby's back until his breathing became regular again. "Gary worked Celeste hard that last year. I think it was the fear of losing her position with the company that made her balk at taking time off for my parents' anniversary. She was on her way to the airport for a sales meeting in Miami when she was killed."

"I remember." Travis's expression had turned solemn.

"He was doing his job. I understand that." David blew out a breath. "But he's the reason she was in that car."

"That's the past." Travis spoke in a low tone. "Over there, in the doorway, is your future."

David glanced in the direction Travis had indicated. July now stood talking with John and Kayla.

"July?" David shook his head slowly. "Sometimes I'm not sure she even likes me."

"She likes you all right," Travis said. "Now it's time for you to decide what you're going to do about it."

July's cell phone rang at three A.M. Instead of being fast asleep like everyone else in the house, she'd been standing at the bedroom window watching the rain fall. She recognized the ring tone and hurriedly picked up the phone.

"A.J." She kept her voice low and glanced at the crib, grateful to see Adam hadn't stirred. "What's up?"

"Does something have to be up for me to call my baby-doll?"

His mock outrage made her smile. The slightly slurred words told her all she needed to know. "Someone has been out partying."

"You know me too well." He chuckled. "When I got home, I remembered what day it was and I had to call."

"Of course." July crossed the room, her mind racing. She slipped out of the bedroom and gently closed the door behind her, trying to figure out the significance of the date.

"Don't tell me you don't remember?"

The hurt in his voice sounded surprisingly genuine. Unfortunately, the days had run together since she'd arrived in Jackson. All she knew was this was Friday...or rather it had been. She hurried down the hall and into the living room.

"Are you kidding?" July glanced at the kid's calendar on the wall. April 11. Since it was after midnight that made today the 12th. "It's our pact day."

April 12, thirteen years ago had been a low point in both their lives. The foster home where they'd been staying had been okay —as far as foster homes went—but July had gotten word she was going back to live with her mother again. Adam was being sent to detention for fighting.

"We vowed we'd show 'em." July spoke softly. "We'd survive."

"Not just survive," A.J.'s voice grew loud. "Overcome."

"Absolutely." Despite the reason A.J. had given, July knew he wasn't calling because of their childhood pact. Something was on his mind. "How's Selina?"

"Missing me," he said, his voice filled with satisfaction. "She called me earlier. We had some great phone sex."

More information than she needed to know, but at least it seemed there was no trouble on that score. "How's the musical? You're in Kansas City this weekend?"

"Omaha," he corrected. "The crowds have been good but I've heard some rumblings that we won't continue touring after this season. I'm not worried."

The heck you aren't.

July knew this man, knew his insecurities. Now she knew why he'd called. "I wouldn't worry either. You're a fabulous actor and dancer. Whenever you stop this tour, you'll get yourself another, bigger role. You've done so well for yourself."

"We both have," he blustered. "Especially for two kids who grew up without a home."

"We had a home," July kept her tone light. "A lot of different homes."

"Houses, July, not homes. We had a lot of houses, but never a home." A.J.'s voice grew loud again and she heard a guy in the background yell at him to keep it down. "How's the baby boy doing?"

"He's fine." July didn't even blink at the abrupt change in topics. Growing up with A.J. had taught her to expect the unexpected.

"Take good care of him." The intensity behind his words puzzled her. "It's not easy being a kid."

A.J.'s voice broke and July realized he must be drunker than she'd first thought. It took a lot of beer to get A.J. emotional.

July's heart rose to her throat, finding his emotion contagious. "I'll do my best by him."

"I know you will." A.J.'s voice lowered. "I gotta go."

July clicked off and sank into a nearby chair. She meant what she'd said to her old friend. She'd do her best by Adam.

If she only knew what that was…

CHAPTER ELEVEN

July didn't sleep much the rest of the night. The worry followed her into the daylight hours. She told herself she'd be a good mother to Adam. She would.

He'd smiled at her again today, really smiled. Oh, Mary Karen had said it was a gas bubble. But when his dark blue eyes had locked on hers and his lips had turned up, there had been a connection. Adam knew her. Adam loved her.

Her head told her that her baby would be better off with his dad. David could give Adam so much more than she could, and not just materially. But how could she walk away from her child? Perhaps shared custody was the answer.

The thought buoyed her spirits for a few seconds. She would find a permanent job. Granted there weren't many options in the area but her upbringing had taught her how to live cheap. Adam could split his time between her and David. It wouldn't be ideal but lots of kids did it. At least he'd have his father and his mother…

We had lots of houses but no home.

A.J.'s words taunted her.

An ache filled July's heart. She remembered the feeling of

never belonging anywhere. If she and David shared custody, would she be dooming Adam to the same fate?

It was time to get to know, really know, the father of her child. And she still had to tell him the truth.

That meant instead of pushing David away, she was going to have to get close to him. With her days in Jackson Hole slipping away, that needed to happen sooner than later.

Despite knowing July had found a new place to exercise, David returned to the Elk Refuge on Saturday. Like many early mornings in April, the temperature hovered just below freezing. David hoped the clean, crisp air would help clear his thoughts. Last night he'd realized how attracted he was to July. Not just on a physical level either.

He rounded a bend in the road and skidded to a stop, unable to believe his eyes. The last person he thought he'd see stood stretching by the side of the path. "July. What are you doing here?"

She straightened, not appearing the least bit surprised to see him. "Waiting for you."

David tilted his head; not sure he'd heard correctly. "Wait a minute. You were waiting for me?"

She flashed a smile. "I thought it'd be fun to walk with you this morning. If you don't mind."

"Yes. No. I mean I don't mind." He took a moment to compose himself. "Walking is a good break for me."

There. At least that didn't sound like a gawky teen in the presence of his latest crush.

"Great." She started hiking down the road.

In several long strides he was beside her.

"I was thinking," she said when he pulled alongside her, "that it might be fun if we did this every morning."

"Really?" He stumbled but caught himself. Her rapid turn-abouts were giving him whiplash.

"Yeah." She kept her gaze focused on the road ahead. "I enjoyed the last time so much I thought it'd be fun to do it again."

Was she talking about the exercise or the kiss? His body stirred at the memory of her sweet lips on his. Still, he didn't want to presume too much. "Sounds good."

"Okay, then." Something that looked a lot like relief crossed her face. "Got big plans for tonight?"

"I'm going to a hospital fundraiser at the Country Club." David knew he should feel more excited about the event, but he couldn't seem to drum up much enthusiasm. Still, he was getting out and that was a first step.

"Dinner?"

"Followed by a dance," David said. "There's also a silent auction and a fashion show by staff."

A mischievous glint filled July's eyes. "Are you modeling?"

"Absolutely not." That's where David had drawn the line. As a member of the medical staff, he was required to attend, but parading across the stage…no way.

July picked up the pace. "Do you socialize a lot?"

"Only what's required," David said. "After your remark the other day, I'm trying to change."

July slanted him a sideways glance. "What did I say?"

"Basically you told me to get a life."

"I did not say that."

"It's okay." David smiled. "You were right. I've been going through the motions for way too long. I'm ready to start living."

The entrance to the Refuge was in sight. While walking with David had given July additional insight into his character, more time was needed. She had to figure out a way to get him to ask her out. Maybe as she became more comfortable with him, she'd be able to be honest about Adam's paternity.

Unfortunately, she'd spent so much time pushing David away

she wasn't sure that would happen. She slanted a sideways glance at his handsome profile.

The clock was ticking. In a couple weeks her assignment would be completed and she'd have a decision to make about Adam's future.

One thousand yards…

"About this event tonight, can people bring dates?"

"Of course," David said, sounding surprised. "The event is open to the community."

Though she wasn't much for big fancy galas, this would be the perfect opportunity for some one-on-one time with David. Seeing him in a tux would be an extra bonus. July slowed her steps and turned to face him. "I was thinking, if you aren't already planning to go with someone, can I come and be your date?"

She braced herself for an enthusiastic yes. Maybe even a hug. She waited. And waited. And waited.

His eyes locked with hers. "I wish I'd known this last week before—"

July's heart sank to her toes. A sick feeling took up residence in the pit of her stomach. "Before?"

"Before I asked Madi Oliver to go with me."

July took a sip of juice and peered over the top of the glass at Mary Karen. She'd been waiting since she walked into the kitchen for just the right opportunity. With the baby fed and Mary Karen's boys still sleeping, this seemed to be it. She lowered the glass and forced a casual tone. "Did you know your brother is taking Madi Oliver to the hospital fundraiser tonight?"

Mary Karen dropped a bagel into the toaster, pushed down the lever and turned to face July. "I'm happy to hear that—" She paused and her gaze searched July's face. "That's not good?"

"No, it's great." July shoved her bowl of raisin bran aside, no longer hungry. When David had told her he had a date—okay so maybe he hadn't called it a date--it had been all July could do to keep it together.

Not because she cared who he dated, but because she felt like a fool for assuming she could beckon and he'd come running.

"July?" Mary Karen dropped into the chair next to her. "Are you interested in dating my brother?"

July resisted the urge to shush her. Granny stood outside the kitchen window mulching the rose bushes, and they both knew the woman had ears like a bat. Instead, she lowered her own voice and forced a casual tone. "I might be."

If "dating" was the only way to resolve her dilemma, then yes, she was definitely interested.

"That's wonderful." Mary Karen's lips parted in a wide smile.

"Did you somehow miss the part where I told you he's taking Madi to the dance?"

"They're just friends." Mary Karen's hand brushed the air in a dismissive wave.

"She's very pretty." July sighed. "And sweet."

"Trust me." Mary Karen met her gaze. "There's nothing between them."

"I was looking forward to going to the event," July said, realizing it was true.

"It's always fun." A wistful expression crossed Mary Karen's face. "I used to attend every year."

"Even if David would have wanted to go with me, I wouldn't have had anything to wear."

Mary Karen brought a finger to her lips. "I have something that would work."

"It doesn't matter." July told herself she should be in the jeep with her camera beside her, heading for the mountains. Instead, she remained in her seat, nursing a barely warm cup of coffee. "I'm certainly not going by myself."

"I could go with you." Mary Karen's voice grew stronger with each word.

July's heart picked up speed but she wasn't going to get too excited. Not yet anyway. "What about a babysitter?"

Bless Granny's heart but watching four boys under the age of five would be asking too much.

Mary Karen's smile faltered for a minute, then brightened. "Esther Wilkins from church is recently widowed. Her grandchildren live out of state. She's told me more than once how much she'd love to watch the boys."

"That takes care of your sons," July said. "What about Adam?"

"She loves babies." Mary Karen's eyes now sparkled. "You can trust her with him."

"Are you sure she can handle four little boys?"

Mary Karen chuckled. "I should hope so...she raised five of her own."

July smiled. "What are we waiting for? Give her a call. Then you can show me the dress."

CHAPTER TWELVE

July resisted the urge to bolt. The lobby of the Spring Gulch Country Club had been decorated with dozens of fresh flowers. But it was the men in tuxedos and women in evening attire that made July want to turn tail and run.

The atmosphere was so far removed from what she'd known most of her life, she felt as if she didn't belong.

"Everyone looks so beautiful," July whispered to Mary Karen as they stood in the doorway surveying the scene.

"They look beautiful," Mary Karen whispered back, "but you look stunning."

July flushed with pleasure at the unexpected compliment. The Kelly-green cocktail sheath fit like it had been made for her. Mary Karen admitted she'd bought the dress several years ago at a closeout sale without trying it on. Not only was it too small, the color was all wrong for her skin tone.

Mary Karen's black dress may have been simple but it hugged her curves in all the right places. It wasn't just the dress. July had been used to seeing the young mother fresh-faced with her hair pulled back in a pony tail. She'd never have believed the difference make-up and some curls could make if she hadn't seen the transformation with her own eyes. When Mary Karen had walked out of the bedroom earlier in the evening and whirled around, even little Logan had started clapping.

"You're the stunning one," July told her.

Mary Karen laughed. "I'd say we both clean up pretty good."

July smiled and felt some of the tension leave her shoulders. "Dinner isn't for almost a half hour. Shall we check out the silent auction?"

Mary Karen waved to some friends across the foyer. "Sounds like a plan to me."

The tables with the silent auction items filled the perimeter of a large room just off the country club's foyer. A huge rustic stone fireplace served as the focal point for the room. Chandeliers made out of antlers hung from the angled ceiling. Though the room teemed with people, because it was so open and airy, July didn't feel crowded.

She made her way down the tables, but nothing caught her eye until she saw the ring. The large heart shaped moonstone held by two carved silver hands immediately jumped out at her. She paused and scanned the information on the item.

"Do you know there is a whole history tied to these Claddaugh rings?" she said over her shoulder to Mary Karen. "How you wear it even has significance."

"I didn't know that." The deep masculine voice reached her ears just as July caught a hint of familiar cologne.

Her heart rate skyrocketed and she whirled.

David--not his sister--now stood behind her. The only trouble was, he wasn't alone.

"Hello, Madi." July smiled. Just like Mary Karen, the woman's simple black dress accentuated her fair complexion. "You look lovely this evening."

"Thank you, July." Madi glanced down at the dress and gave a self-deprecating laugh. "This is quite a change for me."

At the hospital her hair had been pulled back. Tonight, the dark strands hung loose to her shoulders.

"What were you looking at?" David peered over her shoulder.

"A moonstone ring," July shrugged. "Pretty, but way out of my price range."

"I have a friend whose husband gave her one." Madi's pink lips tipped upward. "It's supposed to represent both love and friendship."

"What should be at the core of most marriages," David said lightly.

"I'm sure someone will be happy to get it." July shifted from one foot to the other, feeling very much the third wheel. Then she noticed that although David stood next to her, he wasn't touching her.

The dark cloud hanging over her head vanished. "Have either of you bid on anything?"

David nodded. "I put my number down on a couple items, but it's early. It's impossible to know if I'll be the highest bidder or not."

"I was going to bid on a ski package—" Madi paused. "Can you excuse me for a moment? I better do it now before I forget."

David started to follow but she waved him back. "Stay and talk to July. I won't be long."

He shoved his hands into his pockets. "I guess you're stuck with me."

"I guess I am." July ducked her head and gazed down at her peep-toed heels.

"How've you been?"

"Since this morning? Good." She lifted her gaze. "How about you?"

The silence lengthened and July cursed the awkwardness between them.

"This isn't a date." David met her gaze, his eyes intense and very, very blue. "Madi and I came as colleagues, nothing more."

The electricity was back, snapping and lighting up the air between them. Was he aware how absolutely sensational he looked and smelled tonight? How could he not with all the women in the room casting admiring glances his way?

"It doesn't matter." July's smile felt frozen. "You're free to date who you want."

"It'd matter to me if you were here with a date," David admitted. "I'd hope if you were interested in dating, I'd be the one you'd think of first."

Was this the opening she'd been waiting for? Had her invitation this afternoon opened a door she thought had been slammed shut?

"It might be nice to go out now and then." July kept her tone offhand, determined to let David make the next move. "It probably would be easiest if it was with you. Since we already know each other and all..."

"I'll call you." His eyes never left her face. "Set something up."

"If you want to—" she lifted a hand. "If you don't—"

"I want to take you out on a real date." He reached out for her arm. "I have since—"

"I got the bid in," Madi called out happily and slipped past July to stand beside David.

His hand dropped to his side.

"I thought bidding stayed open until ten." July took a step back.

"It does," Madi confirmed. "But I didn't want to space it off."

"I can understand that." July kept her gaze focused on Madi and avoided looking at David. "I'd better find Mary Karen. It looks like we'll be sitting down for dinner soon."

Even as she spoke the crowd began moving into a great hall filled with large round linen-clad tables.

"You could sit with us," Madi offered. "That way David won't have to sit alone when I'm on the stage."

"On stage?" July cocked her head. "Are you the emcee?"

"Don't laugh." A hint of pink colored Madi's cheeks. "I'm one of the models."

July's blank look must have alerted Madi that more explanation was needed.

"There's a fashion show during dinner. The models are all hospital staff." Madi slanted a sideways glance at David. "They tried to get everyone to participate but David's 'no' must have been a lot more convincing than mine."

"You should have done it." July punched David playfully in the shoulder. "Support the hospital and all that."

"You're absolutely right." The dimple in David's left cheek flashed. "What was I thinking?"

"I'll be expecting you up on that runway next year, mister," July shot back then realized she wouldn't be here for next year's show. Heck, she wouldn't even be here next month. Her smile faded.

"There you are," Mary Karen's heels clacked across the hardwood. "Hello, David. Madi."

"Why little sister I almost didn't recognize you." David took a step back and studied Mary Karen. "You look amazing."

"Yes, she does." Travis' voice sounded from behind July.

July stepped aside and he took a step forward.

A smile of welcome lit David's face. "I'd given up hope of seeing you tonight, Trav."

"Unexpected c-section." Travis shrugged. "What else is new?"

David glanced around. "Where's your date?"

"Let's just say she didn't appreciate being put on hold for another woman…even if that woman was ready to deliver."

"I suppose you can sit with us," Mary Karen drawled. "We don't care that you're a pathetic loser who can't get, er keep, a date."

Madi gasped but Travis burst out laughing. "I don't see you here with a date, MK, so I wouldn't talk."

"I have a date." Mary Karen slipped her arm through July's.

Travis shook his head. "Doesn't count—"

July watched and smiled.

"Children, they'll be no arguing at the dinner table," David said and July could hear the laughter in his tone.

"Your sister called me a pathetic loser," Travis protested.

"He intimated I can't get a date," Mary Karen shot back, her eyes shining with good humor.

"Stop." David held up a hand. "After dinner you can argue all you want. Or better yet, you can kiss and make up."

The two exchanged a glance but didn't respond. Still July noticed that when Travis took his seat at the table, he sat next to Mary Karen.

July wondered if her friend was aware of his interest. Then she noticed the flush in Mary Karen's cheeks and the sparkle in her eyes. She knew all right. July hid a smile.

The waiter had just brought their drinks when Madi excused herself to get changed for the fashion show. With Mary Karen and Travis fighting, er flirting, that left July with David.

"You should wear a tux more often," July told him, keeping her tone light. "You look good."

"I can't wait to get it off." David ran a finger around the inside of the starched collar. "Give me jeans and a flannel shirt any day."

"I know what you mean." July smiled. "I can't wait to take this off."

"As beautiful as you look in that dress." David lowered his voice and leaned close. "You'd be even more beautiful out of it."

The dark flicker of want in his eyes told her he was remembering her naked. Just like that she was back in the hotel room. Even after all these months, that night was still so vivid. The image of him permanently seared into her brain. They'd left the lights on. And they'd taken their time...looking, admiring, tasting and caressing.

July's nipples pressed against the bodice of her dress and an ache filled her belly. She forced her attention away from his lips.

"Do you think I'm a bad mother because I left Adam home with a babysitter tonight?"

A look of startled surprise skittered across his face. Whatever he'd expected her to say, it obviously wasn't this.

Instead of tossing out a glib answer, he took a sip of tea. Then he shook his head. "The way I see it, parents need to make time for themselves."

It made sense but July wanted more. "Let's say the roles were reversed and you were a single father. There are some conservative "experts" who say if you're single, you shouldn't date at all until the child is grown. Others say if you don't take care of your own needs, you can't be a good parent. Which viewpoint do you support?"

Waiters in white dinner jackets swept into the room holding large silver trays. David waited until they'd placed the salads on the table and moved on to answer.

"I fall somewhere in the middle." He stabbed a piece of lettuce with his fork. "I think being so focused on your child that you don't keep yourself open to adult experiences isn't good for either of you. But to do whatever you want, without regard to your child's needs is--in my estimation--wrong."

CHAPTER THIRTEEN

"It's not easy being a parent," July said with a sigh.

"For some maybe." David covered her hand with his and gave it a squeeze. "You're a natural."

She flushed, surprised at how much his approval meant.

Unexpected tears flooded July's eyes. "I love him so much." Her voice broke despite her best efforts to control it. "I only want what's best for him."

"Hey, I may be hassling MK, but at least I don't make her cry." Travis's tone might be light but there was a distinct undercurrent of concern to his words.

Mary Karen leaned close. "Is everything okay?"

"I'm fine." July pulled her hand from David's and swiped the tears from her face with a quick brush of her fingers. She forced a bright smile and pushed back her chair. "I think I'll get some air."

"I'll come with you." Mary Karen began to rise but July put a hand on her shoulder.

"Stay." July met her friend's worried gaze. "I won't be long."

Several people looked up as she wove her way through the tables. Somehow July managed to keep the smile on her lips.

She pushed open the front door and headed down the winding drive. A couple of tears slipped down her cheeks. By the time she reached the golf course, several more had fallen. July leaned against a large shed, feeling like she was teetering on a precipice ready to fall. She could blame the tears on post-partum hormones but July knew it was stress.

She wanted so much to tell David the truth but saying she was sorry to two-year-old Logan this morning had been incredibly difficult. Thankfully he'd just looked at her with those big blue eyes and said "I sorry" back to her. Then he'd smiled.

Yes, she was making progress but not as quickly as she'd like. Still, crying never changed anything, even if it did make her feel better. July straightened her shoulders and took a few deep breaths of crisp mountain air. The tightness gripping her chest slowly eased.

"I know you said you wanted to be alone, but I was worried."

July's heart fluttered. She turned. David stood silhouetted in the overhead light. His shoulders were broad and there was a strength to his face that said this was a man who could handle whatever life threw at him. A man that a woman—and a child-- could count on.

His gaze searched her eyes. "Say the word and I'll leave."

"Stay." Impulsively she took his hand. Although a familiar heat traveled up her arm, it was his strength and comfort that she needed now. "I'm sorry I got teary-eyed. Honestly, before I came to Jackson, I never cried. Lately it seems it's all I do."

"No worries." David's fingers curled around hers. "It's a new mother thing. And, yes, that's a professional assessment."

He said it with such authority she couldn't help but believe him. "That's good to know."

"Mary Karen called and checked on the boys. They're all doing fine, including Adam."

Relief washed over July. "I hated leaving him with someone I didn't know."

"If it makes you feel better, I've known Esther for most of my life. I guarantee Adam is in good hands."

"That's reassuring. I--" The sound of applause drifted from the Clubhouse.

David grinned. "Who knew fashions could be so entertaining?"

July released his hand. "You should go."

David shoved his hands into his pockets, but made no move to leave. "Sick of me already?"

"Not at all." July shook her head. "I just don't want you to miss any more of the fashion show because of me."

"Your exit gave me a great excuse to leave." He shot her a wink. "You realize if we're not careful people may think our departure was staged."

"You meant they'll think you...and me..."

"Exactly."

To July's surprise the thought didn't bother her like it might have only a few days earlier.

"If we go back now, it'll be right in the middle of the show." David rocked back on his heels. "People will really have something to talk about then."

July kept a straight face. "Can't have that."

"I've got an idea."

She had to smile at his excitement. "Tell me."

"We don't go back until it's over." David glanced at his watch. "If the show follows the program, we have a little over thirty minutes. More than enough time for a ride."

"A ride?" July glanced in the direction of the parking lot.

"Not in a car." David gestured to a row of carts lined up inside the open shed. "I'm proposing a moonlight tour of the golf course. Interested?"

July hesitated. "Are you serious?"

"I'll take that as a yes." Within a minute he'd rolled one of the carts onto the wide cement walkway. He held out a hand to her.

"Madame, your chariot awaits."

July took his hand and stepped into the cart, carefully tucking the skirt of her dress beneath her, her earlier tears forgotten. She loved adventures and this night was turning into one.

July curved her fingers around the metal frame. While this was a far cry from a car, the cart was spacious and the padded vinyl seat surprisingly comfortable.

David slipped behind the steering wheel then hit the gas. The vehicle lurched forward.

He kept the cart on a concrete path for a considerable distance before taking off across the grass. The breeze picked up, ruffling her hair. July wrapped her arms around herself. She hadn't noticed the chill when she was standing by the shed but she felt it now. Though the night was mild by Jackson standards, fifty degrees in a sleeveless dress was still cold.

The cart slowed to a stop. David pulled off his jacket and handed it to her. "We can turn back—"

"Not on your life." July slid her arms into the jacket still warm with the heat of his body. "It's so beautiful out here."

Stars filled the clear sky and light from a full moon bathed the course in a golden light.

"I'd heard how big the sky was in this part of the country but I never believed it." She widened her eyes as David hit the accelerator and the cart made its way up an incline. It felt as if they were headed straight up into the heavens. "The night sky and the stars surround you."

The cart eased to a stop at the top of the hill. Above--the sky. Below--perfectly manicured grounds. Light shimmered off the waters of a small pond.

"This is one of the best laid out courses in the area." David sat back in his seat. "When I was in high school, I used to work here."

"You worked?"

"Absolutely." David's tone turned teasing. "Don't tell me you had me pegged as one of those guys who grew up with a silver spoon in my mouth?"

July felt her cheeks warm and she was grateful for the dim light. "Maybe."

He laughed. "My father was a property administrator at Teton Village and my mother taught school. Hardly careers to craft a silver spoon."

A fondness for his parents was evident in his tone.

"I guess I got the idea they had money because of the cruise," July admitted. "I don't know anyone who goes on a month-long vacation."

"This is a first for them as well." David smiled. "The seven-teen-day cruise was their anniversary present to each other. On the way back they decided to stop off in the DC area to do some sightseeing and visit old friends. Once they leave there, they'll stop in Omaha to visit my aunt. By next Saturday they should be back home."

"Sounds like an amazing trip." July fought a stab of envy. "But I'm surprised a teacher could take so much time off during the school year."

"She couldn't have done it if she was still teaching full time." David's expression turned serious. "When Mary Karen's husband left, she took an early retirement to help with the kids. Nothing is more important to her than her kids and grandchildren."

"That's wonderful." July wondered what it would be like to have such a mother.

"Enough about me and my family." David rested his arm on the back of her seat. "Tell me about July. Did you work during high school?"

"I've been working since I was fifteen to help out at home."

A look of concern crossed his face. "I take it your parents were…struggling?"

"My dad wasn't in the picture. My mother is—was--a drug addict. I'm not sure where she is, probably dead." While his mother sounded wonderful, hers could have been the poster child for the need for sterilization. "I was in and out of the house more times than I could count, but they always gave me back to her."

"They?"

"The courts. Judges willing to give her one more chance. Social workers who believed a child belonged with its biological mother." Bitterness laced July's laugh. "For her I was an inconvenience, something that got in the way of her fun."

"Her loss." His arm dropped to her shoulder and he tugged her close. "Is that why you left Chicago? To get away from the memories?"

"The city is more than big enough for both of us. Like I said, I haven't seen her in years." July spoke matter-of-factly. For most people not seeing their mother, not knowing whether she was alive or dead would have been distressing. July knew it was for the best. "I left Chicago because I lost my job and needed work."

"What happened?"

"I was 'reduced in force.'" July shrugged. "It wasn't anything personal."

"I'm sure it wasn't." David offered a supportive smile. "I've seen what you can do with a camera. You've got a discerning eye, a talent for seeing what most people miss."

July pulled the compliment close and wrapped it around her heart. "Thank you."

"You're doing a fabulous job with Adam. Seeing the two of you together, it's apparent that you're going to be a great mom."

"You're certainly free and easy with the compliments this evening." She turned to face him, bringing her lips only inches from his mouth. "I like it."

"I like you," he said in a deep sexy voice that made her bones melt. "I want to kiss you again. If that's okay."

July slipped her arms around his neck and pressed her lips to his, letting that be her answer.

~

A surge of heat shot through David at the taste of her sweet lips. He'd told himself since that day in the Elk Refuge to take it slow. But under the star-filled Wyoming sky with the scent of her perfume teasing his nostrils, slow was no longer in his vocabulary.

He tightened his arms around her, pulling her close, reveling in the feel of her soft curves against him. Just like that night in Chicago he wanted to kiss and touch and make love to her. And then he wanted to do it all over again.

She opened her mouth to his tongue and he plunged inside, his need for her surging to a fever pitch. With his mouth still mated with hers, he slipped his hands up the sides of her dress.

His thumbs had nearly reached her breasts when she gasped and pushed him back.

"What's wrong?" he asked.

"Someone is coming."

He shook his head. "There's no one around for miles."

She twisted in the seat and pointed with one hand. "Then what's that?"

He glanced in the direction and stifled a curse. Less than a thousand yards away—and fast approaching--was a golf cart with its lights on.

"Who do you think it is?" July hissed, straightening in her seat, her lips swollen from his kisses.

"Course security would be my guess." David kept his voice calm and steady which wasn't easy with his body on high alert.

The words had barely left his mouth when the cart pulled up alongside them. David recognized the man immediately. Ron Evans had worked at the course since it was first built. He was also a good friend of David's parents.

David forced a welcoming smile. "Good evening, Ron. What brings you out on the course at this time of night?"

"I was just about to ask you the same question." The burly man's gaze shifted from David to July.

"July is staying with my sister Mary Karen while she's in town." David performed a quick introduction. "Neither of us were interested in watching the fashion show so I offered to give her a quick tour of the course."

"Well, welcome to Jackson." Ron smiled at July then fixed his gaze on David. "Next time let someone know you're taking a cart out."

"Will do," David promised.

They talked for several minutes about the fundraiser before Ron glanced at his watch. "I better get back. I'll leave you two to go back to admiring the stars."

The small smile hovering at the edges of the man's lips told David he hadn't fooled Ron at all. The man knew exactly what they'd been doing before he arrived. Or, if not exactly, then close enough.

"It was nice to meet you, Mr. Evans," July said.

"You too, Miss." The warmth in Ron's tone took David by surprise. He'd always seemed cool around Celeste. Of course, he hadn't really had the opportunity to know her.

"Ron," David said when the man turned to go. This wasn't really the time to speak of it, but their paths rarely crossed. He didn't want another month to go by without saying what he'd meant to say that day. "I didn't get a chance to speak with you at Tim's funeral, but I hope you know how sorry I am for your loss. Tim was a great guy. I know he would have approved of the organ donations."

"Tim loved people." The older man's voice grew thick. "He would have wanted his death to mean something."

The older man shifted his gaze briefly to July and nodded. Then, without another word, he hit the accelerator and in seconds he was out of sight.

"What happened to his son?" July spoke in a hushed tone though Ron was no longer in earshot.

"The day Adam was born, Tim died in a motorcycle accident." David exhaled a breath. "I can't imagine what it would be like to one day have a son and the next day not."

July's eyes filled with tears. "I don't even want to think what that would be like."

It was amazing, he thought, that despite a horrible role model, she'd turned out to be a woman who could shed tears over a man she'd never met.

They sat in silence for several more seconds.

July shifted her gaze from the darkness to his face. "We better get back."

"I need to do just one thing first."

Her brows pulled together. "What?"

"This." He kissed her firmly on the lips, fighting the urge to linger. Then he turned the cart in the direction of the clubhouse and hit the accelerator.

The fashion show was coming to a close when they reached the foyer. July sent David back to the table while she made a detour into the rest room. He'd wanted to wait but she insisted he go back to his seat without her.

Thankfully the ladies lounge was empty. July touched up her make-up then turned her attention to her hair. The cute little up-do Mary Karen had done was now an 'up-and-mostly-down' do.

July grimaced and pulled the pins from her hair. She fluffed the tangled strands with her fingers then stared into the mirror with a critical eye. Definitely more casual but at least she didn't look like she'd been rolling around the backseat of her boyfriend's car on prom night.

Boyfriend.

What would it be like to have David as a boyfriend? For a moment she let herself imagine all the fun they'd have, all the places they could go, all the—

The door swung open. "I thought I'd find you hiding out in here."

July smiled. "Mary Karen, it's not called hiding out. It's called 'freshening up.' David showed me around the golf course and it was a bit humid."

"Humid?" Mary Karen's disbelieving look made July smile.

"How was the fashion show?" she asked before Mary Karen could come up with any more questions.

"Fabulous," Mary Karen gushed with unexpected enthusiasm. "Lots of beautiful outfits."

"I'm sorry I missed it."

"No you're not." The blonde laughed. "You'd much rather have been 'surveying' the golf course with my brother."

"Perhaps." July tried to play coy, but her smile gave her away.

"No 'perhaps' about it," Mary Karen teased. "The hickey on your neck is a dead giveaway."

"Hickey?" July gasped and leaned toward the mirror, scanning her neck and upper chest region for a red blotch. After several seconds she straightened. "I do not—"

She turned to find Mary Karen chuckling.

"You may not have one," Mary Karen said with a sly smile. "But that response tells me you very easily could have had one."

July opened her mouth to deny it, but instead just smiled back.

CHAPTER FOURTEEN

David was surprised when Mary Karen and July said they wanted to stay for the dance. Though she'd complained of being tired earlier, Madi made no mention of wanting to leave when the band took the stage.

Two hours later, after he'd paid for his silent auction items and danced numerous times with not only Madi, but July and Mary Karen as well, the women were finally ready to head home.

"I'm glad I stayed." Madi leaned her head back against the seat of his Suburban.

"It was fun." David smiled, realizing he meant it. "I hadn't heard some of those songs since high school."

"Your sister seemed to be having a good time." Madi slanted a sideways glance. "She and Dr. Fisher make a nice couple."

"They're not a couple," David said, though he had to agree the two looked like they belonged together out on the dance floor.

"They might not be dating." Madi's lips curved into a slight smile. "That doesn't negate the chemistry between them. They definitely have it. You and July have it, too."

"July and I—"

"You don't need to deny it." Madi reached over and touched

his arm. "You were the perfect escort tonight and I had a wonderful evening. But when you look at July—and when she looks at you—well, it reminds me of when my husband was alive. I'm happy for you."

"July and I aren't dating." Even as he protested, David thought of all the time they'd spent together recently. If that wasn't dating, he didn't know what you'd call it.

"It's okay to take a chance."

"What do you mean?"

"I'm saying someone special doesn't come around very often in life," Madi said. "When they do, it's worth taking a risk."

~

David realized as he drove home that he was in love with July. He didn't just want her for one day or one night or even one year...but for a lifetime. Adam, well it didn't matter if the baby was his or not, he already loved the child like a son.

Now all he had to do was find out if July felt the same—

Once he'd stripped out of the tux, he fell into a deep, dreamless sleep. Until the ringing of his phone split the air. Muttering a curse, he slid out of bed and stumbled across the room to where he'd tossed his phone.

He answered without looking at the readout. "Dr. Wahl."

"David, this is Gary. I hope I didn't wake you."

David glanced at the clock on the bedside stand and widened his eyes. He couldn't remember the last time he'd slept until nine. "No. I was awake."

"Good."

David could hear the relief mixed with a healthy dose of nervousness in the man's voice. He wondered if he'd been too hard on the guy. Sure, Gary had been a demanding boss, but he'd given Celeste a lot of opportunities. Even if the hours were long and that last year she'd been on the road more than she was home, Celeste had loved her job.

"—next week. Would that work?"

"Hold on a second, Gary." David grabbed a robe from a hook in his closet and tossed it on. "What were you saying about next week?"

"I'll be in Jackson on Thursday. I wondered if we could meet for a few minutes. Grab a cup of coffee somewhere?"

For some reason, getting together was very important to the guy. Gary had attended Celeste's funeral—had come all the way from LA for the service--but they'd only spoken briefly.

David remembered how distraught Gary had been, almost as if he blamed himself for Celeste's death. The way David saw it, the accident could just have easily happened on his wife's way to the store. The fact that she was on her way to the airport for a business meeting wasn't relevant.

He'd wanted to tell Gary that the day of the funeral but there had been too many people, too many friends wanting to express their condolences. By the time the crowd thinned, Gary was gone.

Despite not wanting to revisit the past, David figured the least he could do was give the guy thirty minutes of his time. "Barring any big emergencies, I should be out of the hospital by four," David said. "Will that work for you?"

"I'll make it work," Gary said.

After finalizing plans to meet at a little bistro on the edge of Jackson, David hung up. Something in his gut told him that meeting with Gary would give him closure on that part of his life. Then he'd be free to open a new chapter…with July and Adam.

CHAPTER FIFTEEN

"I like having Uncle David with us." Connor looked up from his spaghetti and focused his attention on his mom. "Can he eat here every night?"

"I like Unca David, too," Two-year old Logan said loudly, his face covered in sauce.

Mary Karen smiled at her brother. "Your uncle is welcome to eat with us anytime."

"Are you coming tomorrow night?" Caleb asked.

"'fraid not, buckaroo." David looked up from feeding Adam his bottle. "I have a staff meeting at the hospital."

"What's a staff meeting?" Conner asked.

"Lots of talking. Not much getting done." David chuckled and his gaze met July's. The promise in his eyes sent a rush of warmth throughout her body. "But I'll definitely be over afterwards."

Ever since last Friday night, they'd spent all their free time together. David would come over in the evening and they'd eat dinner together. Then they'd take the boys to a nearby park, giving Mary Karen some alone time.

With each passing day, July found herself falling more and

more in love with him. Now, seeing her tiny son in his arms had her heart swelling with emotion. *You have to tell him.*

Soon, she vowed. Soon.

"Hey," David whispered. "You okay?"

"Just a little tired." She leaned her head against his shoulder. "It was a long day."

"Tomorrow night you'll be able to take it easy." He winked. "I won't be here to bug you."

She leaned over and brushed a kiss across his cheek. "I like having you around."

"July kissed Uncle David," Connor called out.

Caleb wrinkled his nose. "Yuck."

July just laughed. Anytime David held her hand or put his arm around her shoulders, the boys had the same response. "Did you tell your uncle where we're going tomorrow?"

"To the movies," the twins yelled.

David smiled but concern filled his eyes. His gaze shifted to his sister. "Tell me you're going, too."

Mary Karen shook her head. "I'm helping Granny write her speech for Sunday. She and her friends are dredging up old memories over dinner tonight. Tomorrow we're going to put them in some semblance of order."

He focused back on July. "What time is the movie? I'll be done by six thirty--"

"We're going at five." She placed a hand on his sleeve, warmed by his concern. "Don't worry. We'll be fine."

"You know you can call me," he said in a low tone meant for her ears only. "Anytime."

Of that July had no doubt. The man sitting beside her was someone she could trust. Someone she could count on. Someone who deserved the truth.

She swallowed a sigh. David hadn't brought up the matter of the paternity test in a long time, but she was sure it wasn't ever far from his thoughts.

He deserved to know that the baby who lay cuddled against his chest was his son. And she needed to be the one to tell him him...not some impersonal test.

Yet now there was an added fear holding her back. Would he want anything to do with her once he learned she'd withheld the truth? How could she bear it if he walked away from her?

~

Instead of taking A.J.'s midnight phone call in her room, July grabbed a blanket and made her way to the front porch and the old-fashioned swing. After several nights in the thirties, the forty-four-degree temperature made the air feel practically balmy.

The stars hung low in the clear sky and the light from the moon cast interesting shadows on the lawn. A breeze ruffled her hair and July wrapped the blanket more closely around her.

She listened as A.J. talked about all the parties he'd attended since he'd gotten his new gig. Parties held by artists she recognized and admired. For her, that crazy lifestyle no longer held any appeal. The life she was living now was the one she'd longed for since she'd been a child.

A home. A family. A circle of friends. How could anyone want for more? David was her Prince Charming and Jackson Hole her fantasyland.

"How's it going between you and the doctor?" A.J. asked.

"I love him, A.J." July sighed into the phone. "Truly, madly, deeply."

"Have you told him Adam is his son?"

A.J. always had been a get-to-the-point kind of guy.

"Not yet," July retorted. "Have you told Selena you love her?"

"Touché," A.J. shot back. "Actually, I confessed my love to a stuffed bear this week, so I think I'm ready to move to the next level."

"Seriously? That's gre—"

"I'm just screwing with you." He laughed. "I'll say it to her, but not over the phone. We have a break next week and I'm flying to Chicago. I'll take care of business then."

"You're waiting for the right time," July murmured, nodding her head. "Just like me."

"I'm waiting to say it in person," A.J. said pointedly. "There's a difference."

"I know." July tightened her fingers around the phone. "It's just that things are going so well between us that I don't want to mess it up."

Silence sat between them for a heartbeat.

"Think about it," A.J. said. "Can you really have a great relationship with that kind of lie between you?"

That same question had tormented July. She leaned back in the swing and gazed up into the heavens. "I'm just so scared."

"What's the worst that could happen if you tell him?"

July thought for a moment. As she'd gotten better acquainted with David, she'd realized that, unlike her mother, David was incapable of physical abuse. "Screaming. Yelling. Telling me what a horrible, weak person I am. Saying he never wants to see me again."

Merely creating the vision escalated her fear. Her heart pounded and her breath grew ragged.

"What's the worst that could happen if you didn't?"

It wasn't a question she'd expected. As she contemplated the possibility, a familiar tightness filled her chest. "The secret will ruin our relationship."

"Sounds like you don't really have a choice. You have to come clean." A.J.'s voice softened. "I know it's going to be hard. Remember, no matter what happens, I'm here for you."

Something in her friend's tone said he wasn't hopeful of a positive outcome. A fresh wave of despair washed over her. "This is going to end badly, isn't it?'

"Quit thinking the worst," A.J. chided. "It could go great. He might say 'no big deal' and you two can ride off into the sunset together...or whatever people do in Wyoming."

It *could*. He *might*. Although July still held out hope, she'd had enough dreams go south to know never to bank on *could* and *might*. Those words were long shots...and she'd never been the lucky sort.

Still, hope was all she had. Hope that David would forgive her. Hope that there *could* be, *might* be, a happily-ever-after in their future. Most of all, hope that she could forgive herself for ruining both their lives if he ended up walking away.

~

The sun had started to set when July drove into Jackson the next afternoon. It had been a long day made even longer by the fact that she hadn't got much sleep the night before.

After her talk with A.J., she'd tossed and turned until almost two. All she could do was think of David and how she didn't want to lose him.

Thankfully driving to Yellowstone and spending the day looking for grizzlies and their cubs kept her mind occupied. She'd gotten some good buffalo and moose shots but it wasn't until she was hiking back to the jeep, that she'd seen the bear and her two babies. July had been far enough away to be safe, but close enough to get some fabulous pictures. The lighting had been perfect. Since she'd been upwind, the animals hadn't even known she was there.

Time had flown by. Though she'd gotten out of Yellowstone far later than she'd planned, July felt good about what she'd accomplished. The photos would finish up this assignment on a high note.

On her way out of the park, she tried to call Mary Karen to tell her she'd be late for supper, but the call wouldn't go through.

It didn't surprise her. Cell reception in Yellowstone was notoriously unpredictable.

She finally reached Mary Karen when she passed through the south gate. Only when she heard Caleb in the background did she remember her promise to the twins. Mary Karen told her not to worry but July knew the boys had to be disappointed.

She thought about stopping to get them some candy to try to make up for missing the movie but by the time she pulled into Jackson it was Adam's feeding time.

Parking the Jeep in the driveway, July grabbed her equipment and hurried inside. The minute she opened the door she heard Adam. His loud "I'm hungry" cry echoed throughout the house.

After quickly unloading her equipment on the foyer's side table, July turned toward the kitchen and her hungry son. She'd only taken a couple steps when Caleb appeared. The smile that normally lit the little boy's face was nowhere to be found.

"You promised to take us to the movies," he said, his blue eyes flashing.

For a second July was struck speechless. She'd assumed Mary Karen had told the boys why she was delayed. From the belligerent look on Caleb's face that obviously hadn't happened.

"I got stuck in the park taking pictures of a momma bear and her cubs." July gestured to her camera. "Later, after I feed Adam, I can show you the photos of—"

"I don't want to see your stupid pictures." Caleb lifted his chin and took a step forward. "You promised to take us to the movies."

The venom in his voice took her by surprise. July stumbled back as if she'd been struck,

He took another step. "You lied."

Was it only her imagination or was the boy growing larger and more menacing with each step?

Tell him you're sorry.

July opened her mouth. For a second nothing came out. But somehow the words made their way past her dry throat and she was able to shove them past her lips. "I'm sorry, Caleb. I promised and I should have been here."

Her triumph at being able to apologize was short-lived.

"I hate you." Caleb leaned forward; his hands now clenched into fists at his side. "I thought you were my friend but you're just a big fat liar. I—"

"Enough." David clamped a hand on the boy's shoulder.

July stared in surprise. She hadn't realized David was even in the house.

"But she—" Caleb protested.

"Not one more word." David clenched his jaw and held onto his temper with two hands. He couldn't remember the last time he'd been so disappointed in one of his nephews.

He'd been in the kitchen with Mary Karen, trying to soothe a very fussy Adam when he'd heard the front door open. He'd handed the baby to his sister and hurried from the kitchen to greet July. He'd only caught the last part of her conversation with Caleb. But he'd definitely heard enough.

While he understood the boy's frustration—after all this had been the second time in less than a week that a movie had been promised but not delivered—there was no excuse for the way the boy had spoken to July.

David shot July a reassuring smile before turning his attention to Caleb. "Son, you need to apologize."

"I won't." The boy squirmed beneath his firm hold. "Me an' Connor wanted to go to the movies real bad. She cared more about her stupid bears than she did about us."

A couple tears slipped down July's cheeks and David cursed the insensitivity of four-year-old boys.

From the other room, the baby wailed. July's anxious gaze slid in the direction of the kitchen.

"Why don't you go feed Adam?" he said in a soft voice. "Caleb and I, well, we have a couple things to discuss."

July didn't argue. With a look of relief on her face, she rushed past him.

Once she was gone, David scooped his nephew up in his arms and took him into the living room where he placed him on his knee. "You and I need to have a talk, man-to-man."

"What about?" the boy mumbled, his gaze focused on his shoes, his lip jutting out.

"Look at me, Caleb." David waited until the boy's eyes met his before continuing. "The way you talked to July was totally unacceptable. I know you're upset, but she apologized. Would you like it if you said you were sorry and I talked to you that way?"

Caleb paused for a long moment then shook his head.

"Would you like it if I told you I hated you?"

"But she--"

"Would you like it if I said that to you?" David said again, this time in a firm tone.

"No."

"How do you think it made her feel?"

Caleb shrugged.

"I can tell it made her feel pretty bad. It'd make me feel awful if you said it to me."

"But she--"

"There is no excuse for that kind of behavior," David said.

"But—"

"No excuse," David repeated. "Do we understand each other?"

Caleb hung his head and nodded.

David gave his nephew a hug. "You're a good boy, Caleb. You have a very loving heart. I know you can do better."

Unexpectedly, Caleb flung his arms around David's neck and laid his head against his chest. "I'm sorry."

"It's not me you need to apologize to," he said softly.

Caleb shook his head and buried his face against David's chest. "Can't."

David stroked his nephew's hair. "A man does what needs to be done."

He turned the boy around and put him on the floor then smiled encouragingly. "You can do it. I have faith in you."

David followed Caleb to the kitchen where July sat at the table burping Adam.

Mary Karen opened her mouth but David shook his head in warning.

Like a prisoner approaching a guillotine, Caleb took a few steps toward July, stopping several feet from her. Pride rushed through David when the boy lifted his gaze and looked her in the eye. "I'm sorry I said those things. I don't hate you."

For a second David feared July wasn't going to respond to the boy's overture. Then her lips lifted in a wobbly smile. "I forgive you, Caleb. Will you forgive me for forgetting about our movie date?"

David held his breath.

"I guess," Caleb said finally. He looked back at his uncle. "Can I go now?" Caleb asked, looking back at his uncle.

"May I go now?" David gently corrected.

"May I go now?"

"Yes, you may."

The words had barely left his lips when the boy raced from the room.

Mary Karen lifted a brow. "What was all that about?"

"Just another day in paradise." David shook his head and chuckled. "One thing I can say about your household, dear sister; it's never dull."

CHAPTER SIXTEEN

After she finished feeding Adam, David suggested they put the baby in his new Ergobaby carrier and take a walk downtown. July really wasn't in the mood to go out. But it was almost the boys' bedtime and with her and David out of the house, Mary Karen could get the boys to bed and help Granny with her speech without any interruptions.

Though the temperature was still mild by Jackson standards, July made sure Adam was bundled up and grabbed a coat for herself. They walked in silence for a block until July brought up the subject still weighing on her mind.

"I hated that you had to get in the middle of that thing with Caleb," she told him. "I'm an adult and a mother. I should have been able to handle a disgruntled preschooler."

"You did fine." David reached over and took her hand. "But I was glad I was there."

"Why?"

"Caleb is smart, but strong-willed," he said. "Mary Karen does a great job with him. But sometimes a boy needs a father figure to reinforce what she's already taught him."

"He was right about one thing," July said with a sigh. "I had promised."

"There is no excuse for a child to speak to an adult in such a disrespectful manner." David's tone brooked no argument. "Not only that, you'd apologized and explained why you were late."

Her heart gave a little leap. "Are you saying a person should always accept an apology?"

"David. July." John Simpson hailed them from across the street.

David waved and turned to July. "Shall we go say hello?"

July nodded and tucked away her disappointment. She was eager to hear David's response to her question. But she would bide her time and find a way to bring it up later. After all, they'd barely started their walk.

Although John and Kayla had left the baby with Kayla's mother so they could have their first "date night" out, they asked David and July to join them for pizza. The growling of July's stomach provided the answer and a moment of laughter.

They snagged a table in the middle of the popular eatery's dining area. The conversation flowed fast and furious despite the fact that every few minutes someone stopped by to visit.

July enjoyed being part of the foursome. She liked talking babies with Kayla. She liked the way David's arm rested on the back of her chair. She especially liked the way David made a point of introducing her when friends and acquaintances stopped by and how he included her in any conversation. By the time the pizza arrived, July felt as if she was on a first name basis with most of the population of Jackson.

"I swear you guys know everyone in town." She bit into a thick slice of pineapple and cream cheese pizza.

John chuckled. "Jackson isn't that big."

"When you've lived here as long as we have, there aren't many people you don't know." Kayla added.

"That would be nice, I think," July said, resisting the urge to sigh. "Though I like the city, too."

"You're from Chicago, right?" Kayla asked.

July nodded and took another bite of the yummy pizza.

"When will you and Adam be heading home?" John filled July's glass with more soda from the pitcher on the table.

July felt David's eyes on her. They hadn't talked about her leaving since the day after Adam was born. Back when she promised him she'd have the DNA test done before she left town. "I'll be here a couple more weeks."

"I wish you'd stay." Kayla reached across the table and gave July's hand a squeeze. "The book club meetings won't be the same without you. You're the only friend I have who has a newborn."

Friend. Tears stung the back of July's lids. Kayla considered her a friend.

July returned the squeeze. "I'm going to miss you, too."

"Isn't there any way you could stay?" Kayla asked, casting a curious glance in David's direction.

"Maybe." July kept her response deliberately vague. "I'm exploring several possibilities."

"Like what?" Kayla leaned forward resting her forearms on the table.

"Like seeing what kind of positions I could get that would allow me to stay. Stuff like that." July gave a dismissive wave. "It's all very preliminary."

"I hope something works out," Kayla said.

"Me, too." She kept her eyes on Kayla and off David. "Me, too."

~

David waited until he and July were on their way back to his sister's house before he brought up her leaving.

From the beginning he'd known she wouldn't be in Jackson for longer than a month or so. Somewhere along the way he'd lost track of the time. What had she said to Kayla—a couple more weeks? That meant that in as little as fourteen days, she—and Adam--could be gone. The knowledge was a boot-kick straight to the heart. "So you're thinking about staying in Jackson?"

She hesitated for only a second. "Considering it."

David could feel Adam's heart against his chest. Since July had carried the baby on their way downtown, he'd offered to take him on the way home. To David's surprise, July had agreed.

He reached down and adjusted the stocking cap on the little boy's head and felt a warm rush of emotion. The time he'd spent with July and Adam these past few weeks had brought a richness to his life he'd never known. They'd filled the empty places in his heart with joy. He couldn't imagine his life without them in it.

"If you're wondering about the DNA testing," July said when the silence lengthened. "I'm going to do it next week."

David didn't know why the offer disturbed him. After all, this was what he wanted, what he'd once demanded. Maybe it was because he'd begun to equate the test with July leaving Jackson. Once it was done, she'd fulfilled her promise and there was nothing holding her here.

"David?"

"Just let me know when you're ready," he said almost brusquely. "I'll bring the testing vials home with me."

"How about Monday?"

"That will work." David remembered how eager he'd been to find out whether Adam was his son. Now he realized that the love he felt for this little boy didn't have a thing to do with the blood running through Adam's veins.

"Got any big plans for the rest of the week?" July asked.

David twisted his lips. "I'm meeting with Celeste's old boss after work tomorrow."

"Really?" Her head cocked. "What about?"

"I'm not sure." David shrugged. "He called and said he was going to be in town and wanted to get together."

She glanced both ways down the side street then stepped off the curb. "Were you two ever friends?"

"I barely knew the guy." In fact, he could count on one hand the number of times he'd even seen Gary. "He was at a couple of parties we attended when we lived in LA. That's about it."

He took July's arm as they crossed the street, but didn't let go when they reached the other side. Strolling down the sidewalk with Adam sleeping against his chest and her hand in his was pure heaven on earth.

"Are you eating dinner together?"

For a second David wasn't sure what she was talking about then he made the connection. "With Gary? Absolutely not."

He could handle Gary for an hour or so but beyond that, forget it. David had a mental image of the man from their previous encounters. Sharp dresser. Big boozer. And stuck on himself. No, an hour would be more than enough.

"Well, since you don't have plans…"

David lifted a brow. "Yes?"

"Mary Karen and Granny are taking the boys to some children's thing at the Playhouse tomorrow night. I thought I could make dinner for you…if you're interested, that is. I also have something I want to discuss with you, nothing big so don't worry."

"I'm definitely interested." David smiled. "I didn't know you cooked."

"I'm no culinary genius." July favored him with an unexpected grin. "I'd say I know just enough to be dangerous in the kitchen."

"Are you going to tell me what's on the menu?" he teased.

"Nope." A little smile played at the corners of her lips. "I have a couple of specialty dishes I'm considering."

"I have an idea." Though David enjoyed spending time with his nephews, what July had in mind sounded more like a romantic evening for two—or three—if you counted Adam. Which meant his home was a much better alternative. "Why don't I give you a key to my house? You could make dinner for us there."

"What about Adam?"

"I have a crib for when Logan sleeps over." David thought for a minute. "Just make sure you bring diapers."

"Anything else?"

They hadn't slept together since that night in Chicago. "I don't have to go in until the afternoon on Friday so if it works for you, you could sleep over?"

Her cheeks turned a becoming shade of pink. "I'd like that."

"Pajamas optional," he added.

July laughed. "I'm not even going to bring them. I'm betting they'll only end up on the floor."

On impulse David leaned over and brushed her lips with his. "Knowing how you make me feel, I have no doubt you're right."

David couldn't believe what a difference a few minutes could make. All week he'd been dreading Thursday because of the meeting with Gary. Now tomorrow couldn't get here soon enough.

~

When July awoke Thursday morning, she realized that with her photography assignment completed, she finally had some time for herself. Determined to look her best for the all-important dinner with David, she made an appointment at a downtown salon to get her hair trimmed. While there she splurged on a manicure and pedicure.

She returned home to feed Adam then they both took a two hour nap. Feeling renewed, refreshed and ready to face whatever the evening might hold, July packed up the baby and headed to the grocery store.

From the comfort of his car seat strategically placed in the shopping cart, Adam stared up at the fluorescent lights while July checked items off her list. She tossed a bag of mixed green lettuce into her grocery cart and was closing in on the garlic cloves and onions when her phone rang.

July recognized the ring tone immediately. She pulled the phone from her bag and slid the phone open. "Hi, A.J."

"Top of the morn to you, my pretty."

July pulled her brows together at the greeting. "Are you drunk?"

"Now what would make you think that?" he asked, neither confirming nor denying her suspicions.

"For starters it's afternoon not morning. And the Irish Wicked Witch of the West greeting is a dead giveaway."

A.J. laughed uproariously as if she'd said something truly hilarious. "I'm not drunk. I'm just happy."

July added fresh mushrooms and onion to the cart and tried to figure out what might have precipitated his joyful mood. "Today's Thursday," she mused. "That means you're back in Chicago."

"Correctamundo," he said. "Back in the city I love."

"Now I know you're drunk."

"I'm feeling great. Life is good."

July paused. After a second the puzzle pieces began to slip into place. "It's Selena. You told her you loved her."

Something that sounded suspiciously like a giggle burst from his lips. "I did indeed. She said she loved me back. Can you believe it? She loves me!"

"Of course I can believe it." Finding his joy contagious, July couldn't help but let a giggle of her own escape. She hadn't heard her friend this happy since, well, forever. "I'm proud of you, A.J."

"I wish I'd done it a long time ago," he said, suddenly serious.

"You did it now," July said. "That's what matters."

"What about you? How are you and the doctor doing?"

"I'm making him dinner tonight." July snagged a couple garlic cloves then wheeled the cart down the dairy aisle.

"Which one of the meals are you making him?"

July dropped a package of cream cheese into the cart then moved to the sour cream display. "I'm afraid I don't know what you mean."

"You only know how to make two things," A.J. teased. "Which is it? Spaghetti bake? Or stroganoff pie?"

"Perhaps I've expanded my culinary skills while—"

"Hey, it's me you're talking to."

July heaved a resigned sigh. "The beef and mushroom stroganoff pie."

"A Merlot would be a good choice—"

"I'm nursing, remember? I don't drink."

"The doc isn't nursing, so pick up a bottle. The wine will get him good and relaxed for what you've got to tell him."

July kept her tone offhand. "Who says I'm telling him anything tonight?"

"You only cook for one reason," A.J. reminded her. "And we both know time is running out."

"You're right. I'm planning to tell him tonight." July waved to a woman she recognized from the gala at the country club. She lowered her voice even though the woman was too far away to overhear. "I have to tell him, A.J. I feel terrible keeping this from him."

"Then do it, July. Don't think about doing it, just do it."

July had just slid the stroganoff pie in the oven and set the timer when she heard the garage door go up. She glanced at the clock on the wall. Though she hadn't known for sure how long David would be, she certainly hadn't expected him this early.

He raced home because he couldn't wait to see me.

July chuckled. More than likely Celeste's old boss had stood him up.

Thankfully she was ready for him. She'd just fed and changed Adam. Other than sautéing the green beans, dinner was in good sha--

The door leading into the house from the garage flung open so hard it hit the wall. Adam jerked in the infant seat where he'd been sleeping but didn't wake up.

David stormed in the room then skidded to a stop, a look of confusion blanketing his face. "What are you doing here?"

"You gave me a key." July could feel anger rolling off him in waves. She forced a smile though her insides had started quaking. "I made dinner for us."

"I'm not hungry," he snapped.

July took a step back, a sick feeling taking over the pit of her stomach.

David must have realized how his response had sounded because he rubbed a hand across his face and forced a half-smile. "I'm sorry. My bad mood doesn't have anything to do with you."

Something bad had happened. Something really, really bad. The look of pain on his face. The despair in his eyes...

July's breath caught in her throat. "Is Mary Karen okay? The boys? Granny?"

She'd seen them all this morning but that didn't mean anything.

His eyes widened. "Has something happened?"

"No. No. You just seem so distraught. I worried—"

"This has nothing to do with them, either." He slumped into a chair in the great room just off the kitchen and exhaled a heavy breath.

Though his edginess made her want to run for the mountains, it was apparent he was hurting. She had to try to help. July scooted an ottoman close to his chair and took a seat. "What happened?"

He met her gaze. Pain warred with anger in his blue depths.

"Celeste wasn't leaving on a business trip the day of her accident. She was on her way to meet her lover."

July's mouth dropped open. She forced it shut. "Who told you that?"

"Gary." David pressed his lips together and massaged the bridge of his nose with his fingers.

July's head spun as she tried to assimilate the information. "How would he know?"

"He was her lover." David gave a humorless chuckle. "For over a year. No wonder she didn't want to move here. She didn't want to be so far from him."

"He came all this way after all this time to tell you that?" July felt her own anger surge. "For what purpose?"

"Apparently he's in some twelve-step program. One of the steps involves making amends."

"Perhaps he should have just apologized to his wife and left it at that."

"He wasn't married at the time." David leaned back against the chair and exhaled a ragged breath. "I never thought she'd cheat. Never. I would have trusted her with my life."

A cold chill traveled up July's spine. "Is there anything I can do to make you feel better?"

"Just having you here makes everything better." He opened his arms and she moved to sit on his lap. When he wrapped her in a tight embrace, she laid her head on his chest.

"Everything is going to be all right," she whispered fiercely against his shirt, not sure if she was trying to convince him...or herself.

"I know it will," he said, stroking her hair. "Celeste and all the lies and deceit are my past. You and Adam, you're my future."

CHAPTER SEVENTEEN

July snuggled up against David and watched him sleep. She'd volunteered to go home but he'd insisted she stay.

He hadn't said anymore about Celeste. Instead he built a fire and after they'd eaten, they spent the evening talking. Several times she almost confessed, but each time she backed off, telling herself it would be like hitting a guy when he was down. No matter how ready she'd been to confess tonight, this was clearly not the right time.

When they'd made love, corny as it might sound, the connection she'd felt had transcended the physical. She knew in her heart of hearts that she would never love anyone as much as she loved him.

She knew David cared for her, too. She could see it in his eyes, feel it in his touch. The only question was, would it be enough when he discovered his wife wasn't the only woman who'd lied to him?

~

July returned home on Saturday to find the household in an uproar. Mary Karen was hosting an after-church luncheon for Granny on Sunday and it seemed to have finally sunk in that the event was only a day away. With their grandparents back in town, the boys were even more hyper than usual.

"I want you to meet my parents." Taking July's arm, Mary Karen dragged July into the kitchen. "Mom. Dad. This is July Greer, the one I've been telling you about."

Dressed in khakis and a polo shirt, Bob Wahl stood a little over six feet. His sandy colored hair was liberally sprinkled with grey. It was the man's brilliant blue eyes that told July this was David's father. He had an open friendly smile and a business-man's demeanor.

Linda had dark wavy hair just like her son's. She was a petite woman, not much taller than July. Unlike her husband she was dressed more casually in jeans and a cotton shirt.

July wasn't sure what Mary Karen had told them, but while their smiles were friendly, their gazes were definitely assessing.

"I hate to run," Bob said, shortly after shaking her hand. "But the matinee starts in thirty minutes."

"Dad is taking the boys to the movies," Mary Karen explained. "Mom is staying to help me clean and get ready for tomorrow."

"I can help, too," July said immediately. "My day is completely free."

"Thank you." Mary Karen smiled. "I'd forgotten David was working this afternoon."

"You know my son?"

The surprise in Linda's eyes appeared genuine. Whatever Mary Karen had told her mother obviously hadn't included her relationship with David. Not yet, anyway.

"David delivered Adam in the ER," July said simply. "We've become friends."

"He's a beautiful little boy." Linda reached over to stroke

Adam's dark head. "I hope you two will be joining us at my mother's celebration tomorrow."

"Of course, she's—" Mary Karen paused. "You are coming, aren't you?"

"It's a family thing." July's hand fluttered in the air. "I wouldn't want to intrude—"

"Nonsense," Linda said. "From what my daughter has told me, you're like part of the family already. My mother mentioned that you and Adam would be there. I'd hate for her to be disappointed."

July knew Granny wouldn't be the only one disappointed. Though David hadn't mentioned her coming since the original invitation she knew he wanted her there. "I'd love to come. Thank you for asking."

"Why don't you help me clean the living room?" Linda's gaze lingered on the baby. "You can tell me what my son has been up to since we've been gone."

Sitting in church was a novel experience for July. But being there surrounded by David's family made it all the more surreal.

Granny looked beautiful in her lavender dress, a corsage of white rose buds pinned to her chest. Her hair had been freshly permed this week and Mary Karen had helped her with her make-up in the morning. Bob and Linda sat beside her then Mary Karen and the boys followed by David, July and Adam. The pews behind them were filled with David's cousins and an assortment of aunts and uncles.

The opening hymn sounded and July rose along with David and the rest of the congregation. David had taken the baby when they'd sat down and hadn't yet given him back. The sight of her son nestled in the crook of his father's arm brought tears to July's eyes.

She couldn't help wondering what it would be like to go to bed with David every night and wake up beside him every morning? To celebrate holidays together? To raise her son as part of this loving family?

The rest of the service passed in a blur. Everyone clapped when Granny got her service award. The little boys started to cheer until Mary Karen shushed them. When Granny thanked her family, for a second July felt as if she were one of them. Until she realized she wasn't part of this family, not really. And she might never be...depending on how David took the news this evening.

Telling him tonight wasn't optimum, especially coming so close on the heels of his wife's betrayal, but she couldn't delay any longer. Not only had she promised to do the DNA test tomorrow on Adam, her job in this area was completed and there was no longer anything holding her here.

Only David.

Maybe it was because she was in a church. Maybe it was because the lie had never weighed heavier on her soul. Whatever the reason, July found herself folding her hands and bowing her head.

Dear God. Please let David understand and forgive me. You know how sorry I am. You know how much I love him. Please, please...

"July," David's whisper was warm against her ear. "Everything okay?"

July popped her eyes open and smiled. She slipped her arm through his. "Everything is perfect."

She only hoped she could say the same thing after this evening.

～

They couldn't have ordered a better day for a party. With an abundance of sunshine, temperature in the mid-seventies and very little breeze, the celebration had been quickly moved out doors.

David whistled as he helped his father set up the tables normally reserved for garage sales. The women put the food out the second the tables were up. With the baby strapped to her front, he noticed July was right out there helping, laughing and talking with his mom and sister.

Celeste had hated coming to family events, claiming she had little in common with his relatives. Most of the time she'd scheduled her work trips when the events had been planned. Now he had to wonder if her unease with his family was simply an excuse. Perhaps she just preferred to spend weekends with her lover.

His heart twisted. He'd thought Celeste loved him. Sure they'd had their issues--what married couple doesn't?--but he'd never thought she'd cheat.

Gary had taken full responsibility for the affair but Celeste had chosen to step outside her marriage vows. Why...?

"July seems like a nice woman."

His father's words jerked David back to reality.

"She's great." He found her across the yard talking to his Aunt Bethany and let his gaze linger. She'd confessed to him on the way to the church that the stretchy brown dress she had on was one she'd worn while she was pregnant with Adam. Since she didn't have much money, she'd jazzed it up with a wide belt covered in brightly colored stones.

Celeste may have been stunning, but David preferred July's quiet beauty. It was more real, just like the woman herself. Someone a man could trust.

"You seem quite fond of her and her son."

Was there a warning in his father's tone?

"I am fond of her." David pulled his gaze from July and shifted his focus back to his father. "You have a problem with that?"

"I don't want to see you rush into anything." His father shifted from one foot to the other. "Mary Karen told your mother that July has already spent the night at your place and—"

"For goodness sake, Dad, I'm a grown man. I don't need lectures about my love life."

"This isn't all about you, David." His dad blew out a frustrated breath. "The woman just had a baby. She's emotionally vulnerable. And there's the father of the baby to consider. He—"

"I'm Adam's father," David said, the words right and true on his tongue. Even if it turned out that he wasn't Adam's biological father, the baby was his son in every way that mattered.

"How?" The look on his father's face would have been funny at any other time. "When? I mean, you've never spoken of her."

"She and I met when I was in Chicago last summer," David said. "For me, it was love at first sight."

He hadn't realized until now what had really been going on in that bar in Chicago---he'd been falling in love.

"I'm happy for you." His father's brows drew together. "But if you two love each other, why have you been apart? And now that you have a son together, why aren't you married?"

"July had a pretty bad childhood," David said, trying to keep things general. "She's a little gun-shy. I think she wants to make sure I'm the real deal before she commits."

"Makes sense." His father nodded and stroked his chin. "I'm just surprised your sister didn't mention anything to your mother."

"Mary Karen doesn't know." David shoved a croquet stake into the ground. "I'd appreciate it if you'd keep this to yourself for now."

"How long?" His father lowered his voice. "You know your mother has this sixth sense for secrets."

"I'm only asking you to hold onto the information until next weekend."

"I should be able to handle that—"

"David." His mother's voice rang out over the sea of people. "Could you go inside and get the twins? It's too nice a day for them to be watching television."

David nodded then turned back to his father. "Say nothing until next week."

"Mums the word."

David knew it wouldn't be easy for his father to stay silent. Hopefully he wouldn't have to keep the secret for long. Tonight David planned to ask July to marry him and to let him be Adam's father.

He smiled as he made his way to the house. This was going to be the start of a new life for him and July. One built on love and trust.

David found himself whistling as he headed inside to look for the twins. He located Connor in the kitchen with a handful of cookies and a guilty expression. He sent the boy outside.

He finally found Caleb in the living room. He wasn't sure what the boy was up to but as soon as David had entered the room, Caleb's hand went behind his back. There was tape on the coffee table and pieces of envelope.

"What's going on, Caleb?" David forced a casual tone. The boy was up to something, that much was certain.

"Me and Connor were just doing some taping."

"What were you taping?"

"Paper."

"Paper like what you have behind your back?"

"Maybe."

"Okay, Caleb." David took a seat on the sofa. It was almost time to eat and he needed to get the show on the road. He didn't want to leave July out there alone with his relatives, no matter how nice they might be. "Tell me what's going on."

"You'll be mad."

"Just tell me."

"I was supposed to be watching Logan yesterday when Mommy was on the phone." Caleb's brows pulled together in a worried frown. "The mailman came and put the mail through the door. Logan went to get it—"

"And--," David prompted.

"Logan ripped open the envelope." The words came rushing out. "I told Mommy we didn't get any mail."

"You know it's not right to lie."

"I was scared—"

"Of what?"

"Mommy made me promise I'd watch him. I let him get the mail. I didn't want her to yell at me."

"Your mommy doesn't yell."

"Sometimes she does."

"That's still no reason not to tell the truth. You understand?"

"Yes sir." Caleb hung his head.

"I'm proud of you for telling me." David tousled the boy's hair. "I want you to promise me that tonight, once everyone has left, you'll tell your mom."

"What about the en-velope?"

David held out his hand. "Give it to me. I'll see what I can do with it."

Caleb whipped the envelope out from behind his back and slapped it in David's open palm.

"Thanks, Uncle David," Caleb raced toward the back of the house. "I'm gonna go play with Connor."

David smiled and shook his head. Raising children wasn't easy. He didn't know how Mary Karen managed on her own. Thankfully, if July accepted his proposal, Adam would have both a mother and a father.

He glanced down at the envelope. This wasn't junk mail. This looked official. And from the address crossed off the front, it had already been all the way to Chicago and back.

As he studied the torn envelope a pink sheet of paper with a raised seal dropped to the floor. He bent over to pick it up and realized it was Adam's birth certificate.

The hospital and delivery date and time were on there along with July's information. His heart stopped beating at the sight of his name and demographic information.

"I'm Adam's father," he murmured. He dropped into a nearby chair, trying to wrap his brain around the paper in his hand.

"There you are." July's cheery voice faded. "The food is on the table—"

She stopped. "What's wrong?"

"You tell me." He flung the certificate on the table. "You read this and tell me what's going on."

The room closed in around July. Murky grey replaced the light. She reached over and snatched up the paper.

The moment her gaze landed on the raised seal, she knew. She opened her mouth to explain but nothing came out.

She'd seen hurt and anger and pain in David's eyes Friday night. She saw all those emotions again now. Only this time she was the cause.

"You knew he was my son all along, didn't you? Yet you lied to my face. All these weeks you continued to lie. Why?"

July stood frozen. Her lack of response seemed to fuel his anger.

"What about the DNA test? Was that another lie? Were you going to leave town without having it done?" His voice grew louder. "Were you going to take my son away and never let me know he was mine?"

July took a step back. First one. Then two. Her heart slammed against her ribs.

"You're not sorry at all, are you? You're just like Celeste. You played me for a fool. The funny thing is I loved you. Heck, I even wanted to marry you."

For a second his expression crumpled and all she could see was the pain.

Reach out to him, she told herself. Tell him you're sorry.

"Why did you--?" he stopped himself. "I have to leave. Tell Mary Karen that I, oh hell, tell her whatever you want. You're good at making things up."

Without another word he spun on his heel.

"David," she finally managed to croak out. "Don't go."

It was too late. He was already gone.

CHAPTER EIGHTEEN

"He hates me," July said to A.J., keeping her voice low so she wouldn't wake Adam, asleep in his crib. She'd been surprised when he'd answered his phone on the first ring. She was tempted to say it was divine providence but after today, she didn't believe in providence, divine or otherwise.

"Did you explain?"

July swallowed hard. She would not cry. She would.not.cry. "He didn't give me the chance."

"He didn't give you the chance? Or you didn't take the chance?"

July had called A.J. hoping he'd make her feel better. Instead she was feeling worse by the second. "I froze up," she admitted. "It didn't matter. He'd already made up his mind that I was in the wrong."

"I hate to tell you, babe, but news flash – you were in the wrong."

"I know." July heaved a heavy sigh. "And I've already been tried, convicted and found guilty. There's nothing more for me to do."

"Ever hear of throwing yourself on the mercy of the court?"

"I don't deserve mercy." Her heart twisted, remembering the hurt she'd seen in David's eyes before the anger flared.

"Everyone deserves mercy," A.J. said softly. "You have to try, July. If not for your sake, do it for Adam."

"What if David won't forgive me?"

"Life will go on. At least you two won't be apart because of words left unsaid."

July realized he was right. She had to at least try.

"I love you, A.J."

There was a long silence.

"I love ya too, babe."

~

The last person David wanted to see at his door the next morning was his sister. "Who's watching the boys?"

"They're in good hands." Her gaze softened as it searched his face. "You look like hell."

"Thank you. Now if that's all—"

"You might wish that's all." Mary Karen stepped past him and breezed into his house like she owned it.

"You want some coffee?" he said, resigning himself to her presence.

She whirled. "I want to know what's going on between you and July."

Playing dumb had never worked before but David gave it a try. "I don't know what you mean."

Mary Karen rolled her eyes. "Let me refresh your memory. You pull a disappearing act. July goes to her room with a headache. All night I hear her crying."

Though David told himself that July should feel bad for what she'd done, the thought of her in tears ripped his heart open. "Did you know Celeste cheated on me?"

Mary Karen raised a brow at the abrupt change in subject, but otherwise her expression didn't change. "No, I didn't. I can't say it surprises me."

David frowned. "Well, it sure as hell surprised me."

"Celeste hated everything about Wyoming," Mary Karen said in a matter-of-fact tone. "You were too busy establishing yourself at the hospital to notice."

"Are you making excuses for her? Are you saying I was a bad husband? That it's my fault she had an affair?" He couldn't believe his own sister was taking Celeste's side.

Mary Karen met his gaze. He saw compassion in her eyes, not blame. "I'm saying don't play the victim or you won't learn anything from the experience."

"Anything else?" he asked between gritted teeth.

"Steve made his share of mistakes but I made some, too. We had problems. Instead of dealing with them, instead of talking to him, instead of listening to him, I pretended everything was fine."

David paused for a moment. Had he done the same with Celeste? "I thought Celeste and I had a good marriage."

"Maybe you did. Maybe you kept those lines of communication open and it didn't matter. Anyway, there's nothing you can do about it now. Celeste is gone. But July is still here and you can talk to her."

Mary Karen swept past him and took a seat in the living room. It seemed his sister had more to say.

He followed her into the room and sat on the sofa. "July won't talk to me."

"Why do you think that is?" Though Mary Karen was playing the bad cop role to perfection, concern filled her blue eyes. "Did you raise your voice to her? I don't know why, but for some reason confrontation of any kind freaks July out, especially when yelling is involved."

"I may have raised my voice, but she still could have told me the reason—" David paused and raked a hand through his hair remembering the way July had shrank back as his voice had grown louder. "I didn't give her a chance to explain," he admitted. "Not really."

Mary Karen smiled for the first time since she'd walked through the door. "The good news is…tomorrow is an excellent day for making amends."

∼

July glanced at her watch. Before Mary Karen had left to run errands that morning, she'd asked July to meet her for a walk in the Elk Refuge at two.

Although Granny and David's mother were watching Mary Karen's boys, July planned to bring Adam with her. When she'd gotten ready to leave, Linda had insisted she leave Adam. Without the baby to get ready, July had arrived at the refuge earlier than she'd planned. Which unfortunately only gave her more time to think.

She couldn't believe she hadn't responded to a single one of David's questions. Still, she hadn't run. That was a breakthrough for her.

After talking with A.J. last night, July had decided she'd give David a day or two to cool off. Then she'd contact him and explain. Even if he didn't forgive her, hopefully at least he'd understand. He was Adam's father. Her son might not end up with two parents in the same house but he deserved a mother and father on speaking terms.

She sighed and glanced at her watch. She'd sworn Mary Karen had said two o'clock.

Finally at ten past two she heard the crunch of gravel and turned, a smile already on her lips. "I was wondering where—" Her smile froze even as her heart skipped a beat. "David."

"Hello, July."

Perhaps she should have gained comfort from the fact that he looked as bad as she felt. But all she experienced was sorrow that her weakness had caused them both so much unnecessary pain.

He gestured with one hand to the open landscape. "Care to go for a walk?"

Regret rose inside her. This would have been the perfect opportunity for them to talk. "I can't. I'm meeting your sister."

"Something came up," he said, his eyes dark and watchful. "I'm her replacement."

He started to walk and she fell into step beside him. July wasn't sure what was going on but they were together and there were no raised voices or yelling. That had to be a good thing. Right?

"I wanted to talk to you," he continued. "But after how I acted last night I wasn't sure you'd want to see me."

How he'd acted?

July struggled for a moment to find her tongue. She cleared her throat and tried again. "So Mary Karen set us up?"

David slanted a sideways glance. "It was my idea."

"Great minds obviously think alike." She tried to force a teasing tone but the tremble ruined the effect. "I was going to call you tomorrow."

"You were?"

July nodded. For a second the familiar panic rose inside her but she took a deep breath then let it out slowly. "I owe you an explanation."

"I owe you the courtesy of listening." He offered her an encouraging smile.

Her heart began to pound and her mouth turned dry, yet for the first time July knew she could do this. Because standing next to her was David. Her son's father. The man she loved.

"My mother hit me and locked me in a closet for two days when I was nine for being clumsy and saying I was sorry and I haven't been able to say I'm sorry since." The words came out in a rush.

David had been so focused on her, on the green eyes filled with panic--almost as if she was reliving the horrible scene--it took a few moments for her words to sink in. When they finally registered, his hands clenched into fists at his sides. What kind of monster would do that to a child? And not to just any child, to his sweet, gentle July?

He touched her arm but she was lost in the memory and didn't seem to notice. Instead she kept walking, her eyes focused on the distant mountains. Finally she stopped and turned to face him. Unshed tears glistened in her eyes.

"I told you Adam wasn't your son because I thought you were married," she said. "But even if you had been married, you had a right to know. Then I found out you were a widower. I tried to tell you so many times—I wanted to tell you--but I could never seem to get the words out."

David saw the truth in her eyes. The doubts he'd harbored since he'd seen the birth certificate fell like scales from his eyes.

"I went to a shrink--a counselor--and he's been helping me face my fears, to realize that no one is going to lock me in a closet for saying I'm sorry or because I admit to making a mistake." Though she was shaking hard now she determinedly straightened her shoulders and looked him right in the eye. "I'm sorry I continued to let you think Adam wasn't your son. I'm so...so...so...incredibly sorry."

The trembling morphed into a shudder and a couple tears slipped down her face.

"Oh, honey." David took her hand and she let him pull her into his arms. "I'm sorry, too. For so many things. I shouldn't have walked out of your life last year. And when I found the birth certificate, I should have given you a chance to explain. Instead I blew up...which is never acceptable. Heck, I treated my nephew better than I treated you."

July wasn't sure what her situation had to do with his

nephew's but it didn't matter. All that mattered was there were no more lies between them, no more secrets. Except maybe one…

She pulled back, just far enough to look into his eyes. "I love you, David. But I understand if you don't feel the same about—"

Suddenly his mouth was on hers, his arms holding her tight as if he'd never let her go and July didn't have to think, she only had to feel. By the time his lips finally left hers, desire, hot and insistent coursed through her body.

"I have something for you," he murmured, nuzzling her neck.

The long hard length of him was pressed against her belly. She rubbed up against him, cursing the fabric between them. "I bet I can guess what it is."

"Umm, that's for later." He grinned. Releasing his hold on her, he slid a hand into his pocket. When he pulled it out his fingers were in a fist. He slowly turned his left hand over and opened it. Lying in the palm was the Claddaugh ring she'd admired at the silent auction. "This is for now."

July gazed at the beautiful ring and her throat grew tight. Was this his way of saying good-bye? Of letting her know when she walked out of his life, there would be no hard feelings? "Thank you. I'll treasure it always."

He picked up the moonstone in his fingers. "This ring signifies friendship, loyalty and love."

Love? Did he say…love?

"I'm feeling suddenly dizzy." July brought a hand to her head. "Do you mind if we step into the shade for a minute?"

Without a word, he took her arm and propelled her under the large branches of a nearby cottonwood, his fingers immediately moving to her wrist. After a few seconds he looked up. "Your pulse is rapid and irregular."

"That's normal." She braced herself against the rough bark of the large tree and gazed up at him through lowered lashes. "It happens all the time when I'm around you."

He smiled sheepishly. "It happens to me, too."

"It does?"

He took her hand and pressed the palm over his heart.

She looked up at him in wonder. "It's racing, just like mine."

He trailed his knuckles down her cheek oh-so-gently. "Why do you think that is?"

Her heart skipped a beat. Then another. She felt all jittery inside, as if she was facing something momentous. "You're nervous?"

David chuckled. "I'm happy. Excited. Scared. All rolled into one."

She homed in on the last emotion. "Why would you be scared?"

"Because I have something very important to ask you and your answer will determined my future happiness."

He took her hand and the world stood still.

"I love you, July," he said slowly, solemnly. "I love our son. My life is so much richer with you both in it. Where you are is where I want to be. So if you want to move back to Chicago or even to Timbuktu, I'll gladly go with you."

July didn't mean to burst into tears but she did. "But I love it here."

David gently brushed away her tears with the pads of his thumbs and gazed at her for a long moment. Then he took her hand and dropped to one knee. In his brilliant blue eyes she saw utter devotion and an abundance of love. "Will you marry me, July?"

"Marry you?" Once again, she'd been rendered speechless.

"Marry me," he repeated in a soft low tone. "Please."

"I do," July said. "I mean yes, I will."

With a loud whoop, he jumped to his feet and took her left hand, sliding the ring on her finger. It fit perfectly. "I pledge you my fidelity and my friendship, but most of all, my love."

Happiness bubbled up as July gazed down at the ring.

"Forever," she murmured, her voice catching at the wonder of it all.

"Scared?" he asked in a gentle, teasing tone, though she could hear a hint of worry.

She met his gaze. "Only that forever won't be nearly long enough."

A slow relieved smile spread across his gorgeous face. "In that case, we shouldn't waste a second."

He pulled her into his arms and before she could catch her breath, he kissed her. Deeply. Possessively. A kiss that sent waves of promise clear down to her toes.

When she finally came up for air and gazed into those love-filled eyes, it finally sunk in. This was no dream. This amazing man was hers. And today was only the beginning of a long and wonderful life.

Now, if they both had a horse and the sun was low in the sky, this would be the perfect time for them to ride off into the sunset together...

But neither of them owned a horse and the sun was still high in the western sky. So instead July wrapped her arms around David's neck and kissed him again. When he whispered words of love against her mouth and down her neck, she decided horses and sunsets were highly overrated.

Everything she wanted, everything she would ever need, was right here in her arms.

I hope you enjoyed David and July's love story. I can see them having many happy years together.

The next story in the Jackson Hole series, HOW TO ROMANCE A STRANGER, brings together Nick and social worker, Lexi when Nick (a stranger to the area) loses his memory in a skiing accident.

Dive into How to Romance a Stranger and see how Nick and Lexi's new love is threatened when Nick regains his memory. Or keep reading for a sneak peek:

SNEAK PEEK OF HOW TO ROMANCE
A STRANGER

Chapter 1

"Five bucks says he's an undercover prince."

Lexi Brennan stood back and watched the older nurse pull a crumpled bill from her uniform pocket and slap it on the counter.

"He's handsome enough," another RN said. "But I say he's a politician's son. God knows we get our share of them in Teton County."

"Put me down for the undercover prince," charge nurse Rachel Milligan said. "Then we'd better get to work."

The staff scattered, leaving Lexi, one of the hospital's social workers, alone at the nurse's station with Rachel and a nurse's aide. During the five years Lexi had been working at the Jackson Hole hospital, she'd lost a lot of money on these friendly wagers. Last month she'd vowed not to participate in another. Still, she *was* curious. "What are you betting on this time?"

"Our new patient, John Doe," Rachel said. "He's been the topic of conversation since the rescue team brought him in yesterday."

"He is super cute," the aide gushed.

"Mr. Landers's call light is on." Rachel kept her gaze focused on the young girl while handing Lexi *John Doe's* chart. "Would you mind seeing what he needs?"

As the aide hurried off, Lexi flipped through the handful of pages. "Not much here."

Rachel smiled. "When a patient doesn't remember his name or any of his history, it makes for a pretty sparse medical record."

Lexi recognized Rachel's handwriting on the initial documentation. "Looks like you were working in the E.R. yesterday when they brought him in from Teton Village."

"He was lucky," Rachel said, her blue eyes suddenly serious. "He might have lost his memory, but another few minutes under that snow and he'd have lost his life."

"Why skiers venture into the back country is beyond me." Lexi wasn't sure why she found the man's recklessness so disturbing. He certainly wasn't the first hotshot skier to take advantage of the mountain's "open gate" policy. "Anyone who goes through that gate knows they're taking a big risk."

Rachel's gaze took on a sad, faraway look. "Young men in that late-twenty, early-thirty range think they're invincible."

Lexi wondered if Rachel was thinking about her husband who'd been killed several years ago trying to protect a clerk during a convenience store robbery.

"Medically, John Doe is stable," Rachel said after a long moment. "Once you find him a place to stay, he's ready to be dismissed."

Raising a finger to her lips, Lexi considered the available options. "There aren't many motels that will take a man with no money."

"He's got money," Rachel said. "He had a couple thousand dollars on him."

A couple *thousand* dollars? Lexi had twenty-seven dollars in her pocket and that had to last until payday. She pulled her brows together. "Did they find drugs on him?"

"Nope." Rachel laughed. "And his tox screen came back negative. My guess is he's just some rich guy who ran into trouble on the back side of the mountain."

"Well, the money will make it easier to find him a place to live," Lexi said, her mind already flipping through the options. She gathered the chart in her hand and walked the few steps to the patient's room. "I guess it's time to meet Mr. John Doe."

"Prepare to be dazzled."

Lexi paused. "What are you talking about?"

"I forgot to mention the most important part," Rachel said. "Not only does he have money, he's gorgeous. That's why my bet is undercover prince."

Gorgeous. Undercover prince.

Lexi pushed open the door. John Doe's money and looks weren't going to help him get a room. That would take luck and a lot of phone calls. And if the weather reports were accurate, a late spring blizzard was bearing down on Jackson Hole. That meant her focus needed to be on finding this man without a memory a place to stay sooner rather than later.

John had just pulled on his ski pants and had a shirt in hand when a knock sounded at his hospital room door. "Come in."

He didn't bother to look when the door opened, knowing his visitor would be another nurse, wanting to check his pupils and blood pressure. But at the click of heels on the tile, he turned.

The woman striding into his room didn't have on scrubs. Instead she wore a stylish green-and-brown dress with a short green sweater. Her dark hair hung loose to her shoulders in a sleek bob, and her amber-colored eyes were focused on the chart in her hand.

When she finally looked up, her eyes widened. "I'm sorry," she stammered, stepping back. "I didn't realize you were dressing. I'll come back later."

He dropped his gaze to his bare chest then back to the two bright spots of pink dotting her cheeks.

No, he decided, this one was definitely not a nurse.

Her hand reached behind her for the doorknob.

"Don't leave." With one quick movement he pulled the turtleneck over his head, ignoring the fierce ache in his neck and shoulders. That pain, the doctor told him, was to be expected. "There. I'm dressed and ready for visitors."

The woman dropped her hand to her side. She smiled, showing a mouthful of perfect white teeth. "I'm Lexi Brennan, one of the hospital social workers and part of the discharge planning team."

She crossed the room. When she drew close and extended her hand, he inhaled the light floral scent of her perfume.

The grip was firm, her gaze direct. He found himself glancing at her hand—as if it had been his habit—and noted she wasn't wearing a wedding ring.

"Mr.... Doe. I've been charged with finding you a place to live." Her expression was serious and all business. "Somewhere you can stay until you regain your memory."

He thought of a dozen quips that might make her smile again. The trouble was he didn't feel like joking.

This darkness in his head annoyed him. Okay, it had him worried. His rescuers had reported that when they'd pulled him out from under the snow, he'd been talking and joking. It wasn't until they'd taken him to the clinic at the bottom of the hill that they'd realized he didn't know who he was...or even if he'd been skiing alone. Only the news that his transceiver had been the only one emitting signals reassured him.

Still, he wished he knew for certain. "Has anyone showed up?"

A look of confusion settled on the social worker's pretty face. "Showed up?"

"You know…family, friends."

Lexi could see the frustration on his face and hear it in his tone. She offered a sympathetic smile. "They probably haven't heard the news yet. Your ordeal was on local television news last night. My understanding is they plan to run the piece again today. And the hospital is putting together a press release that will be sent out if no one comes forth by tomorrow."

He began to pace, finally stopping at a window overlooking the Elk Refuge. "What am I supposed to do in the meantime?"

Lexi didn't have an answer. She placed her leather portfolio on the closest table and moved to his side. The endless sky had turned cloudy as if picking up on the mood inside the hospital room.

"The forecasters are predicting a blizzard." Lexi held to the tenet that when in doubt talk about the weather. "We don't get many this late in April."

Lexi felt his gaze on her and her body prickled with awareness. He smelled clean, like soap and some other indefinable male scent. Rachel had been right. He *was* dazzling. Standing just over six feet with a lean muscular build and dark hair brushing his collar, he was just the size she liked. Coupled with a face that could easily grace the cover of any magazine, he was one potent package.

"When is it supposed to hit?" he asked.

Lexi faced him. "It's supposed to start snowing this afternoon and continue throughout the night."

"The doctors say there's nothing more they can do for me."

His tone gave little away and if Lexi hadn't been looking directly at him, she'd have missed the momentary flash of fear in his brown eyes.

She offered him a reassuring smile. "Look at this move as the next step on the journey back to your old life."

"I'm certainly not remembering my past by sitting and

looking at these four walls." He glanced around the hospital room. "I'm ready to get out of here."

Lexi wondered if he was trying to reassure her or himself. She couldn't begin to imagine how scary it would be to think of going out into the world with no memory. Her heart softened. "I'll make some calls to hotels in the area. See what they have available."

"Can I help? I mean, it's not like I have anything else to do." He flashed a smile. "Besides, this is my problem, not yours."

Lexi steeled herself against the mesmerizing warmth of those chocolate-brown eyes. "That's kind of you. But finding you a place to stay is my job. And I'm hoping to get you the special pricing the hospital has for patients and their relatives."

"The E.R. doctor said I had a couple thousand dollars on me when I was found." He waved a dismissive hand. "Money isn't an issue."

"It won't be if your family or friends come forward." Lexi chose her words carefully, not wanting to dash his hopes. "But if they take a while, or if your memory comes back more slowly than anticipated, you could run out of money. Then—"

"I understand," he said. "I could end up on the street and out of money. That certainly isn't where I want to be." He grinned and pretended to shiver. "Not with snow on the ground."

Lexi returned his smile, admiring the way he kept his spirits up with such a heavy weight on his shoulders. John Doe was definitely one of a kind.

While she considered herself immune to his physical perfection; his humor, intelligence and level-headed attitude were much harder to resist. But resist she would. Because there was no room in her life for a man, even one as handsome and charming as John Doe.

∾

Thirty minutes later, Lexi sat back, frustration coursing through her veins. "How can they *all* be full?"

The words had barely left her lips when Rachel breezed into the room. Her gaze slid from Lexi to John. "What's the verdict? Where's your new home?"

"It's seems," John said, bestowing that hundred-watt smile on the pretty nurse, "that there are no rooms at any of the inns."

Rachel's eyes widened. She turned to Lexi. "Seriously?"

Lexi raked a weary hand through her hair. "It's the storm. Travelers who were going to move on decided to stay. Others who were passing through stopped and got their rooms early."

Rachel's cornflower-blue eyes began to dance. "Surely there has to be *some* place that wants him."

"Hey, I'm right here in the room," John shot back. "Thanks for making me feel like a loser."

The two laughed and Lexi felt a twinge of something that felt an awful lot like jealousy, but couldn't be.

Still, the nurse looked especially pretty today. Lexi wondered if John preferred blondes. Not that his taste in women mattered to her. Besides, for all anyone knew he could be married with a couple of kids.

"I've got an idea." Rachel turned to Lexi. "What about Wildwoods?"

Lexi shook her head. "When I left for work this morning, all the rooms and cabins were full."

"Mrs. Landers had been staying in the lodge while her husband was here," Rachel said. "The doctor dismissed him early this morning and they headed for home."

"Wildwoods?" John cocked his head.

"It's the B and B where Lexi lives," Rachel said. "Just outside of Wilson. About ten miles from here."

John's brows pulled together. He shifted his gaze to Lexi. "You live at a bed-and-breakfast?"

"That's right," Lexi said easily. "And I cook there on the weekends, too."

When she'd been a little girl standing on a stepstool helping her mother prepare meals, she'd never imagined the skills she'd learned would come in so handy. In exchange for low rent she prepared gourmet meals on weekends and holidays. It cost a lot to live in Jackson Hole and a social worker's salary only went so far.

"Sounds like you're a busy woman." John's gaze lingered. Instead of pity or condescension she saw admiration and something else. The pure masculine appreciation lighting his dark eyes took her by surprise. It had been a long time since a man had looked at her that way.

"So, are you going to call Coraline?" Rachel asked.

"Right now," Lexi said.

Coraline Coufal, the owner and proprietor, answered on the second ring. Lexi explained the situation and then held her breath. She wasn't sure whether to be relieved or distressed when she learned there was one room still available.

"We'll take it." Lexi stowed her phone and smiled at John. "Congratulations. Somebody wants you after all."

Don't miss out on the rest of the story. Grab your copy today!

ALSO BY CINDY KIRK

Good Hope Series

The Good Hope series is a must-read for those who love stories that uplift and bring a smile to your face.

GraceTown Series

Enchanting stories that are a perfect mixture of romance, friendship, and magical moments set in a community known for unexplainable happenings.

Hazel Green Series

These heartwarming stories, set in the tight-knit community of Hazel Green, are sure to move you, uplift you, inspire and delight you. Enjoy uplifting romances that will keep you turning the page!

Holly Pointe Series

Readers say "If you are looking for a festive, romantic read this Christmas, these are the books for you."

Jackson Hole Series

Heartwarming and uplifting stories set in beautiful Jackson Hole, Wyoming.

Silver Creek Series

Engaging and heartfelt romances centered around two powerful families whose fortunes were forged in the Colorado silver mines.

Sweet River Montana Series

A community serving up a slice of small-town Montana life, where helping hands abound and people fall in love in the context of home and family.